THE STONE IDOL

THE
STONE IDOL

Franklin W. Dixon

Illustrated by Leslie Morrill

WANDERER BOOKS
Published by Simon & Schuster, New York

Copyright © 1981 by Stratemeyer Syndicate
All rights reserved
including the right of reproduction
in whole or in part in any form
Published by WANDERER BOOKS
A Simon & Schuster Division of
Gulf & Western Corporation
Simon & Schuster Building
1230 Avenue of the Americas
New York, New York 10020

Manufactured in the United States of America
10 9 8 7 6 5 4 3 2 1

Library of Congress Cataloging in Publication Data

Dixon, Franklin W
The stone idol.

(The Hardy boys mystery stories; 65)
SUMMARY: Their search for an Easter Island idol
takes the Hardy boys to Easter Island and on to
investigate the theft of government material in
Antarctica.
[1. Mystery and detective stories. 2. Easter
Island—Fiction. 3. Antarctica—Fiction] I. Morrill,
Leslie H. II. Title.
PZ7.D644Su   [Fic]   80–21896
ISBN 0–671–42289–8
ISBN 0–671–42290–1 (pbk.)

Contents

1   A Mysterious Advertisement   1
2   A Strange Message   8
3   Aku-Aku   18
4   A Thief Escapes   27
5   Mistaken Identity   38
6   Disguised as Natives   48
7   Downhill Danger   57
8   A New Plan   66
9   Penguin Attack   73
10 The Sno-Cat   83
11 Lost in the Antarctic   92
12 Two Suspects   102
13 Rescued in Time   110
14 Airport Chase   118
15 The Wizard   124
16 Guardian of the Sacred Cave   133
17 The Bird Man   141
18 The Inca Chief   150
19 Explanations   158
20 The Final Clue   167

1 *A Mysterious Advertisement*

"Joe, listen to this!" said Frank Hardy, who was standing at the window holding a newspaper.

His brother was relaxing on the bed with a sports magazine. "What is it?" he asked, looking up. "Yesterday's baseball game at Yankee Stadium?"

"Maybe a game," Frank replied, "but it sure isn't baseball. It's an ad in the *Times*: 'Wanted: A sleuth to investigate a strange mystery.'"

Joe got off the bed and joined Frank at the window. They studied the ad together.

The Hardy boys had just solved an embezzlement case for a New York bank and were in their hotel room trying to decide whether to stay in the city for a few more days or to return home.

"What do you make of this ad?" Frank asked.

Joe shrugged. "Why don't you call up and see what it's about? School vacation isn't over for a month yet, so we have plenty of time to solve another mystery."

Eighteen-year-old Frank pushed a strand of dark hair from his forehead and grinned. "Good idea." He dialed the number while his blond brother, who was a year younger, held his ear close to the receiver so they both could hear.

"South American Antiquities," a woman answered. "May I help you?"

"I'm calling in reference to your ad in the *Times*," Frank said.

"You want to speak to Mr. Kimberley," she replied. "I'll ring him for you."

A man's voice came on a moment later. "This is Kim Kimberley. My secretary tells me you're calling about our ad. You must be a detective."

"That's right, sir. My brother and I are amateur detectives."

"Any credentials?" Kimberley barked.

Frank described the bank embezzlement case they had just solved.

The antique dealer sounded impressed. "I saw the newspaper accounts. They say you boys cracked the case all by yourselves. You're the kind of

detectives I need. Do you want to come to my office for an interview?"

Frank looked inquiringly at Joe, who nodded eagerly. Joe was the impulsive Hardy boy. He liked to plunge into any kind of mystery, while Frank was more likely to figure out a game plan first.

"Well, are you interested?" Kimberley asked impatiently.

"Yes, we are," Frank assured him. "We'll be right over."

"Empire State Building, seventy-fifth floor," the man said and hung up.

The Hardys left their hotel and flagged down a passing taxi. Soon they were riding through the rush of Manhattan traffic amid a din of honking horns and squealing brakes. Crowds of pedestrians crossed at the corners as the lights changed.

"A bit more lively than Bayport," Joe quipped.

Bayport was their hometown, where their father had moved the family after spending years as a New York City detective. Now Mr. Hardy was a famous private investigator who had trained his sons to follow in his footsteps.

The taxi deposited them on the sidewalk in front of the Empire State Building. At the seventy-fifth floor, they found South American Antiquities. In the waiting room, they spoke to the secretary. Smiling, she ushered them into Kimberley's office.

The antique dealer was a short, wiry man with red hair and a red beard. He kept flexing his fingers in a nervous manner.

He's worried about something, Joe thought.

Kimberley motioned for the Hardys to sit in front of his desk.

"I'm a partner in South American Antiquities, a business dealing in art objects from South America and its islands," he explained. "We sell artifacts from such places as the Andes Mountains and Easter Island."

"What's your problem, Mr. Kimberley?" Frank inquired.

"It concerns an idol from Easter Island," Kimberley revealed.

"Wow!" Joe exclaimed. "You mean one of those big stone heads?"

Kimberley smiled. "I'm not talking about the huge stone heads. This is a small figure of one of the ancient gods of the island. It was bought at the branch of South American Antiquities in Santiago, Chile."

"Easter Island belongs to Chile, doesn't it?" Frank asked.

"That's right. We maintain the Santiago office to handle pieces from Easter Island as well as from Chile itself."

"Who obtained the idol?" Joe asked.

"I did," Kimberley declared. "I was in our Santiago office when a Scandinavian collector came in and offered it for sale. I saw it was authentic, so I bought it. Later I showed it to my partner, Charles Bertrand. He agreed that I should take it to New York and sell it to a museum. Easter Island artifacts are much in demand, so it would fetch a good price."

"How did the idol get out of Easter Island?" Joe wanted to know.

"That's a good question," Kimberley said. "I see you boys are aware that the ownership of art objects is often in dispute."

"We've investigated cases for museums and private collectors," Frank admitted.

Kimberley nodded and made a pyramid of his fingers. "So you want to know if South American Antiquities has title to the Easter Island piece. Well, it's all open and aboveboard. The Scandinavian collector gave me this document."

He reached into his desk drawer, removed a paper, and pushed it across the top. It was a copy of an official certificate stating that the idol had been legitimately purchased on Easter Island. Only the name of the buyer was blocked out.

"We can't tell who the Scandinavian collector is," Frank noted.

"He wants to remain anonymous," Kimberley

stated. "I have the original with his signature in my safe. I can produce it should it ever be needed. At this point, I prefer to respect his right to privacy."

"So the purchase was legitimate and you brought the idol to New York," Joe said. "Where's the mystery?"

"But I didn't bring it to New York!" Kimberley spoke up.

"Why not?"

"Well, I put it in my handbag in Santiago. I took the bag to the airport and brought it with me to New York. At customs, I opened the bag for inspection."

"And then?" Joe prompted him.

"The idol was not there! It had been stolen!"

2 A Strange Message

"Someone must have sneaked the idol out of your bag on the trip," Joe suggested.

Kimberley shook his head. "Impossible! I had the bag with me from the hotel to the Santiago airport, where I took it aboard the plane and kept it between my feet during the flight. No one could have opened it!"

"Maybe someone switched bags on you," Frank said. "Someone might have taken yours and left a dummy while you were buying your ticket at the airline counter."

Kimberley shook his head again. "I carried a number of small artifacts in the bag. The others were there when I opened it in New York. Only the Easter Island piece was missing."

"Then it must have been stolen in Santiago," Frank concluded.

"That's what I think!" Kimberley boomed.

"Do you suspect anyone?"

"Not really."

"Did anyone else know you had the idol in your bag?"

"Charles Bertrand, my partner. But he can't be the thief."

Frank shrugged. "Mr. Kimberley, if Bertrand is the only other person who knew about the idol, he's a suspect. Would he have any motive for stealing it?"

Kimberley hesitated. "Well, if I were out of the way, Bertrand could take over the company," he said finally

"But how would the theft of the sculpture get you out of the way?" Joe asked.

"Because I have to account for it. You see, whenever we take a piece from the office, we sign a release for it. I signed one for the Easter Island idol. I'm responsible for it, and I have no idea where it is. I could be accused of stealing it myself!"

"Tell us what happened in Santiago," Joe suggested.

Kimberley squinted as if to gather his thoughts. "I took the piece from our office in my handbag. Bertrand came to my hotel that evening and we discussed the price we might place on it in New York. The bag was in the room, zippered and locked."

"Did you leave the hotel room at any time?" Frank inquired.

"Only once. I had to go down to the jeweler's in the lobby to pick up my wristwatch. I was having it repaired."

"Did Bertrand stay behind?"

"Yes. But I don't know whether he was in the room all the time."

"If he had left, even for a few moments, someone else might have sneaked in."

"I'd like to think so," Kimberley insisted. "I don't like to throw suspicion on my partner."

"The handbag was locked," Joe commented. "Whoever opened it must have had a key. Could Bertrand have made a duplicate of your key?"

"It's possible," Kimberley confessed. "I've often left my key ring lying on the desk in our Santiago office. Anyway, it didn't occur to me to unlock the bag and check the contents at the time. I carried it all the way to New York without realizing that the idol was missing."

Joe looked puzzled. "Since it was stolen in Santiago, why don't you ask the Santiago police to find it?"

"I can't!" Kimberley protested. "I'd be the prime suspect. After all, I had the idol in my possession, and now I can't produce it!"

"So you want us to go to Santiago and investigate?" Frank asked.

Kimberley nodded. "I need someone smart enough to find the idol without any undue publicity. That's why I placed the ad in the *Times*. You boys were the first to call me."

"What does the idol look like?" Joe inquired.

Kimberley took a photograph from his desk drawer and handed it to him.

Frank looked over Joe's shoulder and saw a stone head with eyes like circles, a broad nose, and an open mouth. A fierce scowl distorted the features. The most noticeable thing, however, were the ears, with the lobes hanging down almost on a level with the chin.

"The Easter Islanders did that deliberately," Kimberley commented, pointing to the ears with his finger. "You can see the lobes are pierced. People hung weights on them so they would become enlarged. Of course, the practice has stopped in modern times. But long ears have always been a feature of Easter Island art."

"How big is this sculpture?" Frank wanted to know.

"About six inches high," Kimberley informed him.

"Then it's not heavy. You wouldn't have felt the loss of its weight in your bag."

"No," Kimberley agreed. "I never noticed that the bag was lighter, not with all those other stone artifacts in it. Well now, let's get down to the bottom line. You boys are obviously top-notch detectives. I'd like you to take the case. What do you say?"

The Hardys explained that they would have to talk to their father first.

"Fenton Hardy?" Kimberley queried. "Yes, I saw he was mentioned in the newspaper reports about the embezzlement case you just solved."

"If we take your case," Frank said, "we need a little more to go on besides what you've told us so far—some clue or starting point. We can't just go to Santiago and hope we'll be lucky."

"I have something," Kimberley said slowly. "A strange message I received. Here it is." Again he reached into his desk drawer and drew out a piece of paper, which he handed to the boys.

The message was composed of words cut from a newspaper and pasted on a South American Antiquities letterhead bearing the Santiago address. It read:

WHEN THE MOUNTAINS ARE COVERED WITH
MIST, AND THE FULL MOON IS OVER THE PEAK,
THE IDOL IS SAFE IN THE CAVE.

Frank and Joe looked baffled.

"Mr. Kimberley, where did you get this?" Frank asked.

"And what does it mean?" Joe wanted to know.

"It came in the mail from Santiago," the antique dealer told them. "And I have no idea what it means. But since it mentions an idol, I think it must refer to the Easter Island god figure."

"It's on note paper from your Santiago office," Joe pointed out.

"True. But lots of people have access to that."

"The message must be a clue," Joe stated. "Maybe it came from somebody who knows where the idol is but doesn't want his identity revealed."

"It might be one of our Santiago employees," Kimberley said.

"Well, whoever wrote this is telling us to investigate the Santiago office," Frank declared. "That's where we'll begin if we take the case."

"When can you let me know?" Kimberley asked in a tense voice.

"After we talk to our father," Frank replied. "We'll phone you this afternoon."

When the Hardy boys returned to their hotel, Frank called long distance to Bayport.

Aunt Gertrude, who was their father's sister, answered. "Why aren't you home yet?" she demanded in a tart voice.

"Well, we might have another case, Aunty," Frank said. He knew that although Aunt Gertrude was often critical of her nephews, she was basically proud of their accomplishments.

"Hmph!" Miss Hardy snorted. "Don't you ever give up? Can't you stay home for a change like other boys? Seems to me that if you're not in danger, you're not happy."

"Don't worry, Aunt Gertrude, this case isn't dangerous," Frank said and quickly explained what had happened. "And now may I talk to Dad, please?" he added when he was finished.

"Just a moment."

Fenton Hardy took the phone. "I found out how you solved the mystery," he began. "An old friend of mine in the New York Police Department called me about it."

"It was easy," Frank said modestly.

Fenton Hardy chuckled. "That's not what my friend reported. He considers your performance a remarkable example of detective work. What are you going to do now?"

"More detective work—maybe," Frank announced. "If you think we should take the case."

"What does it involve?"

Frank described their conversation with Kim Kimberley and his request for their services.

Fenton Hardy thought for a moment, then said, "Go ahead. It should be interesting."

Frank detected a slight hesitation in his father's voice. "You sound as if you're not all that happy with the idea."

"Well, I've just taken a new assignment, and I might need your help. It concerns the theft of government materiel from several naval bases. The navy has no idea who the thieves are, and hired me to find out."

"Shall we come home, then?"

"No, not yet. You see, I'll have to tour the naval bases where the thefts have occurred. If I do need you, it won't be until after the tour is over and I've checked out several clues."

His father paused a moment, then went on, "Tell you what. Go to Santiago for the time being, and stay at the Inca Arms Hotel. I'll get in touch with you there if necessary."

After Fenton Hardy had hung up, Joe rang Kimberley's office and told him that they would be able to work on his case, but might have to take time off to help their father.

The antique dealer hesitated for a moment, then

said, "Okay, why don't you come back here and we'll talk about it."

"We'll be right over, sir."

Joe hung up and the boys taxied to the Empire State Building for the second time that day. The secretary showed them into Kimberley's office, and he motioned for them to sit down.

"I'm hoping you'll find the idol before your father needs you," the antique dealer said. "If not, I'm in trouble. But I decided to give you the job anyway because I feel that boys your age will be less conspicuous. You realize, of course, that you can't walk into our Santiago office and tell my partner I hired you to investigate him and his staff."

"We understand, sir," Frank said. "What kind of cover do you have in mind for us?"

"I thought you could be high-school students with a special project in Incan history. You contacted me and I referred you to Santiago, because our staff there can help you study the artifacts we have. You have a research grant from your school to cover your expenses."

"That sounds like a plausible plan," Joe conceded.

Kimberley nodded. "Now here's where you go when you get into town. Our office is on Avenida Bernardo O'Higgins, or as we would say in English, Bernard O'Higgins Avenue."

He handed the boys a card bearing the printed legend of South American Antiquities, with the address and phone number underneath. "And take the strange message and the photograph of the idol with you, too."

Joe took the two items while Frank pocketed the business card.

Kimberley sighed. "I don't like to deceive my partner, and I'm sure he has nothing to do with the theft. But someone in our office must—our staff were the only people who were in on the transaction and knew what hotel I was staying in."

Frank nodded.

"My secretary will give you your expense money on your way out. Call me as soon as you have any news."

"We will, Mr. Kimberley," Joe promised.

"Oh, there's one other thing you should know about."

"Yes?"

"Depending on how you look at it, you might be in danger from the idol's *aku-aku!*"

3 Aku-Aku

Frank and Joe stared at Kimberley in surprise.

"What's an *aku-aku?*" Joe asked.

"An uncanny spirit. The people of Easter Island believe that *aku-akus* watch over them and all their possessions, especially those objects connected with the old religion. If the people obey their traditions, the spirits protect them. But if they step out of line, the *aku-akus* haunt them and bring bad luck."

"The old whammy," Frank said with a grin. "When an *aku-aku* puts a spell on you, you've had it."

"Sounds somewhat like voodoo," Joe commented.

"Right," Kimberley said. "Thor Heyerdahl wrote

a book called *Aku-Aku* about his experiences on Easter Island. He found the people convinced of the power of the spirits. They say anyone who disturbs an idol of the gods is in for trouble. Looks like it came true for me. I've had nothing but headaches since I bought that piece."

"Why are you telling us this?" Frank queried.

"Because you may run into the idol's *aku-aku* before your investigation is over. I don't want to frighten you off the case, but I feel I should warn you."

"We won't be frightened off," Frank promised.

Kimberley nodded. "Good. I've heard you boys aren't afraid of danger. That's why I'm depending on you to find the idol and have whoever stole it from me arrested. When can you leave?"

"On the next available flight," Frank declared.

"That's fine. Solve the mystery as quickly as you can. I'll be waiting to hear from you."

The boys returned to their hotel and discovered that the next plane from New York to Santiago was scheduled for the following afternoon. They spent the night in the hotel. After breakfast the next day, they went to a bookshop to buy a book on Incan art and did some sightseeing. Then they took a taxi to Kennedy Airport. Soon they were airborne, winging their way south along the eastern shore of the United States.

The boys took turns studying the book they had bought.

"We'll have to beef up on the subject," Frank said. "Otherwise Bertrand will never believe our cover."

After dinner was served, both Hardys fell sound asleep and did not wake up until breakfast the next morning. Meanwhile, they had reached South America; the massive peaks of the Andes could be seen below.

After they landed near Santiago, the brothers took a taxi to the Inca Arms Hotel. Large crowds were thronging the streets. Most people wore ordinary dress, but here and there the flash of brightly colored robes showed that Indians from the mountains were visiting the city.

The taxi turned into a broad thoroughfare with a street sign reading "Avenida Bernardo O'Higgins."

"This street's wider than Fifth Avenue in New York!" Joe said, surprised.

A drive of about a mile took them to the Inca Arms Hotel. It was near the building in which South American Antiquities was located. The boys could see the long range of the Andes from the window of their hotel room.

After they had stowed their things away and freshened up, Frank used his high-school Spanish to phone South American Antiquities. He continued struggling with the language when he got an answer on the other end. The man he was speaking to chuckled.

"You can speak English," he said in a jovial voice. "I'm Charles Bertrand from Saint Louis. My receptionist's on vacation, but perhaps I can help you."

"Oh, hello, Mr. Bertrand," Frank said, and introduced himself. "You're the person I wanted. My brother Joe and I are students working on a special project on Incan art. Mr. Kimberley said you might let us study the artifacts you have."

"Kim called me about it," Bertrand said. "I'll be glad to help you. Come on over to my office and we'll talk."

Frank thanked him and hung up. "Bertrand wants to see us, Joe."

"I hope we can check out his office while we're there," Joe said tensely.

The Hardys strolled over to South American Antiquities, which was in a building of ornate Spanish design. They mounted a flight of stairs and saw the name on a door at the end of a corridor.

They walked over and entered the outer office. It was empty. Joe banged the bell on the receptionist's desk with his palm, and a metallic peal sounded from the inner office.

A few second later, the door opened and Charles Bertrand appeared. He was a stout man with a twinkle in his eye. He wore a tiepin decorated with an Incan motif, a vicuña delicately chiseled in gold.

Smiling, he shook hands with the Hardys.

"I'm always glad to meet someone from the States," he declared. "Especially people who are as interested in the Incas as I am. I trust Mr. Kimberley explained what we do here at South American Antiquities."

"Yes, he did," Frank replied.

Bertrand led the Hardys into his office. A number of shelves held pieces of sculpture dating from the Indian cultures that existed in South America before the voyage of Columbus. Behind Bertrand's desk hung a photograph of Machu Picchu, the city hidden in the Andes to which the Incas retreated after the Spanish conquest.

Near the desk sat a tall, dark man with black, piercing eyes.

"Boys," Bertrand said, "meet Julio Santana. He's our chauffeur. By the way, you can speak English to him. He learned the language from American missionaries on Easter Island."

"Easter Island?" Frank's eyebrows shot up.

Santana smiled. "That's where I was born. But I left quite some time ago to work as an oil driller in Punta Arenas down in Tierra del Fuego. Then I came to Santiago and got the job with South American Antiquities."

"We're very interested in Easter Island artifacts," Joe spoke up.

Santana scowled. "Are you selling any?"

"Oh, no! We're students working during our vacation studying Incan art."

Santana smiled and seemed to relax. "You had me worried for a moment. You see, plenty of artifacts have been stolen from my island lately. Many pieces are being sold illegally on the international market."

"I heard about that," Frank said.

Bertrand fingered his vicuña tiepin. "We have no Easter Island pieces here at the moment. But we do have Incan sculptures for you boys to examine."

The conversation continued, and it was agreed that the Hardys would come back to the office on the following day to begin their studies.

Then Bertrand accompanied them through the outer office, which was still empty. This time Frank and Joe were able to survey it more thoroughly than when they entered. They both noticed a photograph on the wall. It showed a section of the Andes covered with mist while a full moon gleamed over the tallest peak.

Opening the door of the reception area, Bertrand ushered the Hardys into the hall. "My secretary will be back in a few days," he said. "She can help you when I'm not here. See you tomorrow!"

With that, he closed the door. The Hardys heard his footsteps as he crossed the waiting room, then the door to the inner office slammed shut.

"Joe!" Frank exclaimed in an undertone. "Did you notice? That photo on the wall fits the message Kimberley gave us!"

"It sure does, Frank!" Joe took the paper out of his pocket and read: " 'When the mountains are covered with mist, and the full moon is over the peak—' "

He broke off with a puzzled look. "That fits all right, but what about the rest? 'The idol's safe in the cave'?"

"Maybe there's a secret compartment behind the picture!" Frank guessed. "That could be the cave in the message. Let's go back in and look. We might not get another chance once the receptionist comes back."

Joe nodded. "Let's hope Bertrand and Santana stay in the inner office long enough for us to check behind the photo!"

Gingerly, the boys opened the door again and slipped into the reception area. They made their way across the room to the photograph of the Andes hanging on the wall.

All the while, they could hear the voices of Bertrand and Santana inside. The two men were talking about making a company car available to a wealthy buyer who would soon arrive in Santiago.

Frank carefully lifted the photograph up far enough to release the wire from its hook. As the wire came clear, the hook snapped upward like a control switch.

Silently a secret panel slid to one side, revealing a small compartment in the wall. The Hardys peered in curiously.

A small stone sculpture with round eyes, a flat nose, and open mouth was staring out at them!

Frank lifted the figure from its hiding place, while Joe pulled the picture Kimberley had given him out of his pocket. The idol and the picture matched perfectly!

Suddenly the door to the inner office swung open and Bertrand and the chauffeur stood framed in the doorway. They stared at the boys in disbelief.

"W-what are you doing there?" Bertrand cried out. "And where'd you get that statuette? My partner took it to New York with him a while ago!"

"He didn't," Frank said. "We found it in this secret compartment!"

"Found it! It seems to me you were about to steal it!" Bertrand thundered. "You have no business snooping around in my office. Good thing we caught you red-handed!"

"I'd say *you're* the one who was caught," Frank replied evenly.

"What do you mean by that?"

"We're turning this over to the Santiago police. Mr. Kim—"

He was interrupted by Julio Santana. "Oh, no, you're not!" the chauffeur snarled and lunged at the boy, snatching the idol from his hand. Reeling from the force of the blow, Frank crashed into Joe and the two fell to the floor.

In a flash, the Easter Islander ran out into the corridor and disappeared!

4 A Thief Escapes

Scrambling to his feet, Frank rushed after Santana with Joe close behind. By the time the Hardys reached the corridor, the chauffeur was already at the stairs. He glared furiously at them over his shoulder, then hurried down to the ground floor. The boys followed, taking the steps three at a time.

Santana rushed through the revolving door and ran up the street. Just then an elderly woman stepped into the door, turning it slowly. Frank and Joe had to wait until she was through before sprinting after the fugitive. However, once in the street, they closed in on the Easter Islander again. Frank was only a few feet away from him when Santana suddenly leaped off the sidewalk. He maneuvered through the traffic as cars jolted to a

halt to avoid hitting him and drivers shouted angrily. Then he wrenched open the door of a taxi and jumped in. The next instant the taxi sped off!

The Hardys looked for another cab, but none was in sight. "We've lost him!" Frank cried disappointedly, as he watched the car vanish up Bernard O'Higgins Avenue.

Joe nodded in disgust. "What do we do now?"

"Stop blocking traffic, Joe!"

Frank had become aware that the blaring horns were aimed at them. One driver leaned out of his window and shook his fist.

Grinning apologetically, the Hardys hastened to the sidewalk and made their way back to South American Antiquities. Bertrand was running up the street, looking wildly for Santana and the boys. When he saw them walking toward him, he stared in surprise.

"You came back?" he panted.

"Of course," Frank replied. "Unfortunately, Santana escaped."

"I thought you three were in with each other," Bertrand declared. "After all, you took the idol out of the wall compartment—"

"Why don't we go to your office?" Frank suggested. "We'll explain everything to you then."

The businessman nodded. "We'll have to call the police," he said, his voice shaking.

"Perhaps not," Frank said. "Maybe you'd like to give us the job of finding Santana."

"Are you kidding? I wouldn't ask a couple of school kids to catch a thief!"

"Mr. Bertrand," Joe said, "we're detectives. Mr. Kimberley hired us to find the Easter Island idol, which he had packed in his bag to bring to New York. When he arrived, it was missing. He felt someone in your Santiago office must have stolen it and suggested that we investigate while pretending to be students interested in Incan art."

Bertrand stared at him, his mouth open. They had arrived at the office, went inside, and the antique dealer sat down heavily behind his desk.

"Now let me digest this for a moment," he said. "You're right. Kim did take the sculpture and signed a release for it. But then, what was it doing in that compartment outside?"

"That's what we'll have to find out," Joe said.

"But how did you know it was there?"

"We didn't," Frank replied. "Mr. Kimberley received a strange message." He pulled the note out of his pocket and handed it to Bertrand. "When we saw the photo in the reception room," he continued, "we decided to look underneath. And there was the secret compartment with the idol in it!"

"I don't understand why Santana snatched it and ran off," Bertrand declared. "He constantly delivers things for us—many of them more valuable than the stone figurine—and he never once stole anything!"

"We'll have to find the answer to that question," Joe said. "Mr. Kimberley did not want the police involved in the case because he feared a scandal. If it's all right with you, we'll try to catch Santana for you."

"Oh, it's all right with me," Bertrand said. "You're probably correct in saying the less publicity we have, the better."

"A thief on the run has to hide somewhere," Frank spoke up. "Have you any idea where Santana might go?"

"Well, he has relatives in an Indian village in the Andes. He could go there."

"Where is it?"

"On a slope of the high peak directly to the east of Santiago."

"Then that's where we'll start," Frank said. "But there are a few things we have to know. For instance, what about that secret compartment?"

"It was there when I rented the office," Bertrand replied. "However, I've never used it as a hiding place."

"Who else knew about it?"

"Kim did, and I suppose some of our employees. There are twelve, including Santana, and of course visitors come and go."

"So, many people had access to the stationery on which the note was printed," Joe suggested.

Bertrand nodded.

"When did you last see the idol, except for just now?"

"The day before Kim left for New York. It was right here in this office. Kim put it in his bag when he went to the hotel. I saw him later in his room. The bag was there and locked, and I figured the idol was in it."

"He told us you watched the handbag while he went to collect his wristwatch," Frank stated. "Did you stay in the room all the time?"

"I went down the hall for ice," Bertrand replied.

"Were you gone long enough for someone to sneak into the room and steal the idol?"

"It's possible. Most of the ice was gone and I had to wait for the machine to make more."

"That's when the thief must have entered!" Joe declared. "Santana could have overheard you talk about the idol earlier, and he probably knew about the secret compartment. He could also have a duplicate key that would unlock the handbag."

"Santana's from Easter Island," Frank observed. "Maybe that's why he wanted the sculpture. He could have shadowed you and Mr. Kimberley to the hotel, climbed up the fire escape, and watched through the window. When you left the room to get ice, he could have entered, unlocked the bag, taken the idol, and escaped."

"Then he hid the idol in the secret compartment in your office until it was safe for him to dispose of it," Joe continued his brother's line of thought. "That's why he hit the ceiling when he saw we had found it. So, he grabbed it and ran off."

"It's just a theory," Frank pointed out. "We'll see if it holds up when we interrogate Santana. But we have to find him first."

"I think you should get right on to it," Bertrand advised.

"We will," Frank said.

The Hardys left South American Antiquities, rented a car, and drove through Santiago. Joe was at the wheel and Frank held a map of the Andes spread out across his knees. Gradually the city gave way to the suburbs, and then they were rolling through the country toward the Andes, the great mountain chain of South America.

Joe broke the silence. "This is a weird case, Frank. We came down here to investigate Bertrand for Kimberley. Now we're investigating Santana for Bertrand."

"It's a switch, all right. And there's no doubt

about Santana's guilt. We all saw him take the statuette."

They went on, mulling over the problem. Soon the pavement beneath their wheels was replaced by a rough dirt road that made the car bounce up and down over large boulders and into deep potholes.

"This ride's giving me a crick in the neck!" Joe complained as he wrenched the wheel to avoid running into a gulch on the right.

"And I just banged my knee on the dashboard," Frank lamented with a grimace, rubbing the injured spot.

When they entered the foothills of the Andes, the road led steeply upward. The air became thinner and colder, and they found breathing difficult.

"If we get any higher, we'll need oxygen masks," Frank joked.

But the road soon flattened out and they were able to catch their breath as they got used to the altitude. They drove along narrow ledges bounded by rocky mountain walls on one side and precipitous cliffs falling away for hundreds of feet on the other.

Suddenly, as they rounded a hairpin turn, they saw another car hurtling directly at them! The road was too narrow for the two vehicles to pass. If they tried, one would go over the cliff!

Frantically, Joe slammed on the brakes. The other driver did the same. Tires screeched on the stone surface of the road, and they came to a jolting stop with their front bumpers nearly touching. A man got out of the other car and walked up to the boys. He was obviously an Indian and shouted something in what the Hardys took to be his native language. Frank shrugged and held his hands up to indicate that they did not understand.

Gesturing in sign language, the Indian let them know that he was going to back up and that they should follow him. Frank nodded, smiling gratefully.

Joe trailed the man's car until they reached a place where the road widened sufficiently to let them pass. They waved their thanks to the Indian, who waved back.

"That was a close shave!" Frank exclaimed. "Good driving, Joe! You stopped just in time or the car would have turned into a pile of junk!"

"Give our friend half the credit, Frank. If he hadn't hit the brakes, he'd have plowed right into us, no matter what I did."

They continued on their route until they saw stones bouncing from a slope above them.

"Watch it, Joe!" Frank warned. "It looks like a landslide's coming our way!"

Joe stopped. More stones hit the road and careened over the side of the cliff into the valley below.

Then a clatter of hooves became audible, and a herd of small, woolly animals with long necks came bounding down the slope.

"Vicuñas!" Frank exclaimed. "There's our landslide!"

The animals, which resembled small llamas, leaped nimbly onto the road and continued over the side of the cliff. Finding footholds on what appeared to be a sheer wall, they zigzagged down the slope and began browsing on the bushes at its base.

Joe resumed the drive. They entered a valley where they saw tents pitched near a trench. A dozen men were digging, and a station wagon parked nearby bore the legend INCA EXPEDITION U.S.A.

"Let's ask them if they know where the village is," Joe suggested and pulled up to the station wagon.

The leader of the expedition came forward. "You look like Americans," he said.

"We are," Frank confirmed. "Frank and Joe Hardy from Bayport."

"My name's Professor Yates. I'm in charge of this expedition. What are you boys doing this far back in the Andes?"

"We're looking for a nearby Indian village on the slope of the tall mountain," Joe informed him. "Can you tell us where it is?"

"Straight ahead, about five miles. Some of the men from the village are working here on our dig. We're excavating one of the main Incan sites in this region, searching for articles of a civilization that flourished centuries ago."

"Sounds fascinating," Joe said. "Have you found any?"

"Oh yes, lots of stuff. What about you fellows? Are you visiting someone in the village?"

Frank nodded. "A man named Julio Santana."

"Julio? What a coincidence. You don't have to go any further."

"Why not?" Joe asked.

"He's right here in our camp!"

5 Mistaken Identity

Frank and Joe stared at each other in amazement. What luck to catch up to Julio Santana so quickly!

"He must have come directly here after he escaped from us," Joe thought. Aloud he said, "Can we see him, Professor Yates?"

"No problem. Come on."

Yates led the way over to the spot where the excavation was taking place. A mound of earth rose beside the trench where the men were working. Figurines, shards of broken pottery, and other archeological discoveries were laid out on a table next to it.

A young woman sat at a table writing in a

notebook. Yates introduced her to the Hardys as Gloria Nemitz from Milwaukee.

"I'm listing all the stuff we dig up," she said. "Each piece gets a number and a description."

"Gloria, where's Julio Santana?" Yates asked.

"He left camp a little while ago. He said he'd be back later on."

"Why don't you wait here till he returns?" Yates invited.

"We'd like to, Professor," said Frank. "We could use a rest."

"You can have chow with us in the meantime."

Joe patted his stomach and grinned. "That's even better!"

Yates introduced the Hardys to the rest of the crew on the dig. Then loaves of bread and cans of food were brought from the store tent, and all sat down on the ground and pitched in.

Gloria Nemitz was next to the Hardys. "Are you friends of Julio's?" she inquired.

"We met him," Joe said evasively, "in Santiago."

"That figures," she said. "He spends a lot of time in Santiago."

Then they began to chat about the Incan Empire that extended through the Andes before the coming of the Spanish Conquistadors. After the meal was over, the Hardys helped clean up. Santana still had not arrived.

"You boys look strong enough to help with the dig," Yates declared. "Want to give us a hand while you're waiting?"

"We'd be glad to," Frank and Joe agreed enthusiastically.

Yates chuckled. "Good. Let's see what you find." He handed Joe a pickax and Frank a spade, and showed them where to work. Joe began cutting a furrow along a line indicated by a cord stretched between two posts. Frank got down in the trench and turned over the earth carefully so as not to break anything he might strike. Other members of the dig worked beside them, lifting the earth out of the trench and adding it to the mound.

After some labor with the pickax, Joe felt his implement strike stone. He scratched away the earth with his hands and uncovered a series of stones in a straight line. Beneath them he came to a second series.

"Professor, this looks like a flight of stairs," the boy called out.

"I thought the steps might be there," Yates commented after surveying Joe's discovery. "That's why I had the cord tied as a guideline. My men can now start excavating the rest of the stairs."

Meanwhile, Frank had been cautiously digging in the trench and uncovered a pot. Using his fingers, he carefully brushed the earth away, removed the container, and held it up. The sunlight gleamed on the representation of an animal with a pointed snout, heavy leather plates around the body, and a long tail.

"I found a pot with an armadillo on it!" Frank exclaimed.

"That's a real treasure," said Yates enthusiastically. "All we had dug up so far were shards, or bits and pieces of pottery. Now we have an intact container. It's an example of armadillo ware from Central America. Shows trade was carried on between Central America and Chile in ancient times. Well, you boys have done enough. Have a rest until Julio gets here."

"There he is!" Gloria called out. She pointed to a pickup truck rolling into the camp. It stopped near the Hardys' car. The boys ran forward and waited expectantly as the driver got out. However, they gaped in surprise when they saw he was a portly man with blond hair and blue eyes!

"Julio, the Hardy boys are here to see you," Yates said. "They've been waiting for you."

"Why is that?"

Frank gulped. "Mr. Santana, we thought you were somebody else. We're looking for a man with the same name. He's from Easter Island and is dark-complexioned with dark hair."

Santana grinned. "I am from Santiago. I deliver

provisions to this camp." He pointed to boxes of food stacked in the back of the pickup.

"You don't know the other Julio Santana, by any chance?" Joe queried.

"No, I do not."

Yates had been listening to the conversation. "A case of mistaken identity, eh?" he said. "That's too bad. And there's no use asking the Indians on the dig about your Julio Santana. They're very close-mouthed with strangers."

"Then we'll have to go on to the village," Frank said. His voice showed his disappointment.

"Well, it's not far," Gloria pointed out sympathetically.

The Hardys said good-bye to their hosts and drove on toward the Indian village. People were tramping along the road, and Frank, now at the wheel, had to slow down frequently to avoid running into one of them.

They were dressed in their native clothing. The men wore rough boots, heavy shirts and trousers, broad-brimmed hats, and ponchos over their shoulders. The women had on colorful skirts, shawls, and aprons. Many of them wore hats with high crowns resembling derbies.

Most people gave the Hardys sullen stares. Some deliberately stayed in the middle of the road and forced Frank to drive around them.

"What's eating them?" he wondered. "What do they have against us?"

Joe shrugged. "Maybe they don't like strangers. Professor Yates said something to that effect, remember?"

At last the Hardys came to the village. They saw a number of wooden houses, but the main square was surrounded by rows of two-story buildings of modern, prefabricated design that looked like military barracks.

"They must have been put up by the Chilean army," Joe guessed.

Just then a tall, muscular Indian stepped in front of their car, held up his hand with a scowl, and made Frank stop. He shouted something to the people in the square, and they began to gather around the boys.

"I don't think we're going to get much cooperation out of them," Joe said apprehensively.

"Looks like a freeze-out for us," Frank agreed. "I don't like it one bit."

The crowd was large and hostile. Some of the men started to push the Hardys' car, which rocked back and forth.

Frank rolled down his window and tried to explain in Spanish why he and Joe were there. But threatening cries drowned out his words, and the Indians rocked the car more violently.

"They're going to turn us over!" Joe cried.

The Hardys braced themselves against the dashboard, while the natives violently tilted the vehicle up on two wheels.

Suddenly an older man pushed through the crowd and shouted something at the Indians. The men let go and stepped aside, as the car fell back on its four wheels with a crash.

"Who are you?" the man demanded.

"Frank and Joe Hardy from Bayport in the United States," Frank replied, glad that the man had spoken English.

The Indian nodded. "I thought you were Americans. I learned your language when I worked for an archeological expedition. My name is Ata Copac. I am the village leader."

"Why are your people so hostile to us?" Joe asked.

Copac smiled. "They thought you were tax collectors from Santiago." He turned and spoke to the villagers in their native language. Their sullen stares turned into pleasant smiles, and a number came up and shook hands with Frank and Joe. Then the men drifted away from the car, leaving the Hardys alone with Ata Copac.

"Why are you here?" the village leader inquired. "Are you tourists?"

"No. We're looking for a man named Julio Santana," Joe explained.

"From Easter Island," Frank put in. "We were told he might be in this village because he has relatives here."

"I know Julio Santana," Ata Copac said. "But he is not here. His village is on the opposite slope of the mountain."

"How do we get there?" Frank inquired.

"Over the mountain pass."

"Then we'd better be on our way. It's getting dark."

Ata Copac shook his head. "You cannot drive. The path is too steep. You will have to go on foot. And you will not find your way in the darkness. I suggest you stay here for the night and set out in the morning. You can sleep in an empty hut."

The Hardys gratefully accepted the invitation. Ata Copac got in the car with them and showed Frank where to drive. The hut was a one-story building with a table, a couple of chairs, and several canvas cots. Blankets were piled on the cots.

"I think you will be comfortable here," the village leader declared. "Tonight we celebrate one of our holidays. Perhaps you will join us?"

"We sure will!" The boys grinned.

When they stepped outside, night had fallen and

torches shone in a field just behind the hut. The villagers were piling up logs in the middle of the field. When they finished, they lit the kindling and an enormous bonfire roared up through the logs.

Women began to roast meat over the fire, and the rest of the feast came from jars of corn, peas, and potatoes. The natives filed past, plate in hand, to get their share of the food.

"Chet should be here," Frank said to Joe. He was referring to their best friend, Chet Morton, who liked eating better than anything in the world.

Frank chuckled. "You're right. Chet could devour all this food by himself."

Ata Copac and the Hardys sat down at one end of a long table set up in the field and pitched into their dinner with gusto.

Afterward, the Indians performed on drums and wind instruments. Frank and Joe found the music strange at first, but after a while began to appreciate the rhythmic beat.

"We could play these numbers at high school graduation," Frank said jokingly.

"And we could cut a disc for our stereo," Joe quipped, "except that we don't have a sound stage. I'd like to have a go at those drums!"

"So would I. They're as good as the ones we have at school."

Frank and Joe were in the band at Bayport High.

They usually played guitars, but they recently doubled on the drums.

Ata Copac put his arms around the Hardys' shoulders. "Oh, please give us a demonstration!"

Then he translated for the villagers. Many voices called out to the boys.

"They want you to play for them," Ata Copac interpreted.

"Okay, let's go, Joe," Frank said. "We can't say no to our public. What'll we start with?"

"The Bayport Rag," Joe suggested.

Taking over a couple of drums from the grinning Indians, the Hardys went into their familiar routine. They began with a low rhythm, and then increased the sound until their drumming echoed over the village. The audience clapped and shouted. They swayed in time to the rhythm, and applauded loudly at the end.

The celebration finished shortly afterward. The boys returned to their hut, slipped under the blankets on their cots, and went to sleep.

A noise outside wakened Joe in the middle of the night. He stepped to the window and looked out. In the moonlight, he could see a man at their car, twisting the cap off the gas tank!

Joe rushed to the door and swung it open. The man heard him and looked up.

He was Julio Santana!

6 Disguised as Natives

Santana darted away from the car, and Joe ran after him. The chase led between rows of barracks-like houses, behind the main store of the village, and across the square.

The young detective strained his eyes in the moonlight to keep Santana in sight. But he was hampered by running in his bare feet. By the time he reached the opposite side of the square, the Easter Islander had vanished into the night.

Joe came to a halt, wincing at the sharp pebbles underfoot. Realizing that any further pursuit was hopeless, he turned and went back to the hut where Frank and he were spending the night. After making sure that no gas had been siphoned from the car's tank, he woke Frank up and told him what happened. The boys decided to take turns standing watch for the rest of the night, in case Santana came back. However, all was quiet until eight o'clock in the morning, when they decided to get dressed.

"Santana must have been watching from the mountain to see if anybody was after him," Frank said as he pulled on his jeans. "He recognized us and tried to put our car out of commission by emptying the gas tank."

"And I'm sure he must be at the other village now," Joe added. "We've got to check him out."

The boys made a breakfast of some army rations they found in the hut. They were just finishing when a knock sounded on the door and Ata Copac entered.

"I have come to give you directions," he said. "You follow the road over the pass, turn right along a cliff, and you will come to a bridge over a deep gorge. Cross the bridge and you will see the village on the other side of the canyon."

"Thank you," Frank said. "And something else has just occurred to me. It would be better if we had a disguise."

"Why is that?"

The Hardys explained about Santana and his theft of the Easter Island idol.

"He might stir up the villagers against us if we

look like outsiders," Frank said, "Or we might be mistaken for tax collectors again."

Ata Copac nodded. "I understand, and I will help you. If Santana is a thief, I wish him to be caught. If you find him with the idol, I will ask his village leader to have him arrested. Now, come with me."

Leading the way to his house, he produced Indian clothing, a wooden washtub, and a bushel basket full of blackberries. The Hardys crushed the blackberries in the water until it became a dark color; then they rinsed their hands and faces to hide their light complexions. Joe also drenched his hair to make it look black.

Next the boys donned rough shirts, trousers, and boots. They slipped ponchos over their heads and pulled broad-brimmed hats down over their foreheads to mask the light color of their eyes.

Joe grinned. "Think we'll pass for Indians, Frank?"

"As long as we keep our hats on. Let's see if these getups work."

Keeping their eyes fixed on the ground, the Hardys walked through the square, mingling with the natives who were dressed just as they were. No one seemed to notice the two Americans.

"Looks as if we can get away with it," Frank muttered. "They can't tell the difference."

"Have your Spanish ready, Frank, in case somebody talks to us," Joe advised.

The Hardys said good-bye to Ata Copac and thanked him for his help. Then they walked along the road beyond the village leading to the mountain pass. Whenever they met an Indian, they hurried by quickly in order to avoid any questions. They followed a narrow, rocky trail up to the pass, where they could see snow-covered mountain peaks in the distance. One huge outcropping towered over their heads.

"That's the cliff Ata Copac mentioned," said Joe, pointing to the right.

He led the way onto a narrow ledge running along the top of the cliff. Frank was directly behind him, and they edged forward carefully.

Suddenly Joe stepped on a boulder that gave way under his foot. Shaken loose, it hurtled down onto the jagged rocks below. Joe clutched wildly at the air in an effort to regain his balance. However, he failed, and with a frantic scream, toppled off the cliff!

Frank lunged forward and reached for Joe's poncho. For a moment, the younger Hardy boy was suspended in the air with nothing between him and the rocks at the bottom of the cliff. Then Frank got a firm grip on the poncho and pulled his brother back to the safety of the ledge.

Joe blew his breath out in a great gasp. "Wow! That was too close for comfort!"

"It sure was, Joe! Don't step on any more boulders. You almost scared me to death!"

Moving cautiously along the cliff, they reached the other side. From there, a short walk brought them to the deep gorge Ata Copac had mentioned. The bridge crossing was made of narrow branches tied with heavy ropes to trees on both sides of the canyon. Two more ropes were strung about three feet above the first pair, and fastened to them at three-foot intervals, providing the handrails.

The makeshift bridge swayed in the wind as the Hardys approached it. They looked down and saw a small stream meandering at the bottom of the gorge.

"You have to be an acrobat to cross over that thing," Frank muttered. "It's a death-defying stunt!"

"I just hope the guy who anchored it to the tree knew how to tie a good sailor's knot," Joe added apprehensively.

Placing a foot on the first branch, and steadying himself by holding onto the handrails, Joe started across. Frank followed. The bridge rocked from side to side as they moved, and the ropes strained at their moorings. The branches creaked under the weight of the two boys.

It was slow going, and their hearts were pounding by the time they reached the opposite side. With relief they jumped onto solid earth.

The Indian village they were looking for lay right in front of them. The people and the buildings resembled the ones they had just left. It was market day, and stalls were set up in the village square. Vendors were selling food, clothing, utensils, and farming implements. A pen held a small flock of vicuñas being offered for sale.

"Joe, let's pretend to be Indians from the mountains, in town for market day," Frank advised. "And keep an eye open for Santana."

Joe nodded tensely. Holding their heads low, the Hardys walked into the throng in the village square. Stall owners called out to them, offering their wares. Shaking their heads to indicate they were not interested, the boys moved on. After a few minutes, they began to feel secure in their disguises.

Suddenly Frank tugged on Joe's poncho and nodded toward a booth where small stone sculptures and other artwork were being offered. A man with his back to them was arranging the exhibit on a table behind the counter.

"Let's take a look at what he's got for sale," Frank said.

Joe shrugged. "You don't expect to find the Easter

Island idol there, do you? Santana knows its worth. He'd never sell it to a guy like that. He wouldn't make any money on it."

"I know. But maybe the vendor can give us a clue as to where one might sell a valuable sculpture."

Casually the boys strolled over to the stall and looked at the pieces on the table. The man turned around with a smile, which froze on his face as he recognized them.

Frank and Joe gaped. He was none other than Julio Santana!

"The Hardys!" Santana exclaimed. "Welcome to our village. Would you like to buy one of my artifacts?"

"Where's the Easter Island idol you stole from South American Antiquities?" Joe demanded.

"Here it is!" Santana replied. He turned and took a small sculpture from the table. With an icy stare, he thrust it into Joe's hand.

The boys examined it. "This is an imitation Incan piece!" Frank declared.

Santana paid no attention. Instead, he screamed in Spanish: "Thieves! Thieves!"

A number of Indians whirled around and stared at the Hardys.

"Thieves! Thieves!" Santana kept yelling. Quickly a crowd began to gather, making threatening gestures at the young detectives.

"Let's get out of here!" Frank hissed.

Joe dropped the sculpture and the boys took to their heels, pushing people aside as they ran past the stall.

When they reached the open area leading to the bridge, a mob of Indians was behind them in headlong pursuit. In Spanish, they shouted threats of how the thieves would be punished once they were caught.

Frank dashed onto the bridge, followed by Joe. Desperately they tried to run over it fast, but the dipping of the branches under their feet and the swaying of the ropes held them up. They were about three-quarters of the way across when Santana arrived at the canyon. He took hold of one of the handrails.

"Grab the other one!" he shouted to a man beside him. "Now, do as I do!"

He moved the rope back and forth, and his companion followed suit. Together, the two men caused the bridge to sway dangerously from side to side.

Frank and Joe clung to the rails as the motion became more violent. High up in the air they fell to the right, then swung clear around to the left. The mountain spun before their eyes, and with each swing, they hovered over the gorge for a split second.

At last the bridge was flung too high for a return swing. It turned upside down and collapsed.

Frank and Joe were thrown off into the deep gorge below!

7 Downhill Danger

As the Hardys flew through the air, their fingers closed around one of the handrails. Gripping the rope tightly, they braked their fall and hung suspended over the gorge. Their Indian hats fell off and drifted down into the stream.

Frank was unable to turn his head. "Joe, are you there?" he called out anxiously.

"Right behind you!" Joe panted.

"Move ahead hand over hand," Frank yelled as he began to pull himself along the rope. Joe did the same.

"They're getting away!" Santana shouted. "They're getting away, and we can't follow them with the bridge turned upside down!"

Frank and Joe reached the opposite side of the canyon and pulled themselves up onto solid ground. They collapsed on the soft earth to catch their breath. Meanwhile, the bridge began to swing again. Staring across the gorge, they saw that Santana and a group of natives were trying to turn it right side up.

"Let's get out of here!" Joe exclaimed. "They'll be coming across in a minute!"

The boys rushed into the underbrush and concealed themselves beneath some tall bushes. They were still too exhausted from their ordeal to run very far. Peering through the branches, they could see the bridge hurtling back and forth in a wide arc. Finally it reached its peak and fell down into its original position.

Santana and his companions ran over it as fast as they could and began to scout through the underbrush for the Hardys.

"We can't stay here!" Frank said in a hoarse whisper.

"We don't have to!" Joe whispered back. He pointed to a spot where a cave extended into the mountainside.

Hitting the ground, the Hardys crawled into the cave and pulled small bushes and twigs over the entrance. Then they lay flat, gasping for breath and waiting to see what would happen.

Their pursuers had split up and were running in all directions. Suddenly Frank and Joe heard Santana's voice. "They got away!" the chauffeur complained in English.

"Perhaps you were foolish to come here," another man said.

"It was an obvious choice. I wanted to stay with you until we could go on."

"It was too dangerous," his companion declared.

Frank and Joe could hear his footsteps as he came closer to the cave. Then they saw the outline of his figure through the brush. He stretched out his hand and the Hardys froze in terror.

Had he discovered their hideout?

But the man only plucked a few berries from a bush, popped them into his mouth, then said, "What will you do now, Julio?"

"I will return to Santiago with the idol and hide out at Ernesto's until you are ready. The Hardys will search the village and the mountains for me and they will never suspect I went back to the city."

"Good," the other man agreed. "I will find you at Ernesto's when the time comes."

Both men walked off. Frank and Joe remained in their hiding place for a long time. Then they finally emerged cautiously, hoping that all the Indians had returned to the village after their futile search.

"Now what?" Joe asked.

"Let's go back to our car and drive to Santiago," Frank advised.

"Too bad we can't follow Santana," Joe said. "But I'm sure he's left already. I wonder where he plans to go with the other fellow."

Frank shrugged. "I have no idea."

The boys followed the return route along the ledge and through the mountain pass. They hurried to the Indian village without encountering any hostile natives, and quickly made their way to Ata Copac's house, where they told him what happened.

"I am sorry you did not catch the thief," the village leader said.

Frank nodded. "Well, at least we know he's headed back to Santiago," he said. The boys thanked Ata Copac for his help and washed off the dark dye they had used to disguise themselves. Then they exchanged their Indian garments for their regular clothes, said good-bye to their host, and drove off with Joe at the wheel.

As they reached the steepest segment of the mountain road, he stepped on the brakes to slow their speed. Nothing happened. The car careened crazily forward!

"The brakes don't work!" Joe shouted.

"And we're going too fast to jump out!" Frank judged. "Keep steering, Joe!"

Gripping the wheel, the boy struggled to stay on course. Rocky walls threatened the Hardys on one side, plunging cliffs on the other! Joe veered around curves at top speed, dodging boulders and potholes, while the speedometer of their car went up and up!

As he rounded one corner, Joe saw another car racing directly toward them. Realizing there was no room for both, he made a split-second decision. Wrenching the wheel to one side, he steered off the road and the other car whizzed past.

The Hardys bounced into an open area and slowed down as the wheels became entangled in grass and bushes. Joe swung around in a circle, and his vehicle gradually came to a stop.

Bruised and shaken, the young detectives stared at one another. Joe mopped his forehead with a handkerchief.

"That was a close call," he said in a trembling voice.

Frank nodded. "I want to look at those brakes. I bet—"

Just then a familiar voice called out, "Are you boys all right?"

Gloria Nemitz came running up, followed by Professor Yates. Without realizing it, the Hardys had reached the area of the American archeological dig.

"I saw you drive off the road," Gloria continued. "It looked like you were in trouble."

"We were," Joe admitted, as he and Frank climbed out of the car. "Our brakes didn't work."

"You can get them repaired here," Yates declared. "We service all our own vehicles."

"Thanks. That's great, Professor," Frank said. "But first I want to find out what went wrong."

He crawled under the car and inspected the machinery. Then he emerged with a grim face. "The connecting rod is nearly filed through," he reported. "It snapped when Joe stepped on the brakes at the top of the hill!"

"Somebody tried to kill us!" Joe exclaimed.

"But who would want to do that?" Gloria questioned.

"Julio Santana, the man from Easter Island," Frank replied, and described their adventures since their visit to the dig, and the reason they had come to Chile.

"I'm sorry to hear you have such a dangerous assignment," Yates said. "Why don't you walk over to our supply tent? We've got spare connecting rods."

The boys accepted his offer and repaired their car.

"Why don't you stay for some food?" Gloria invited when they were finished.

Frank shook his head. "Thanks, but we can't. We have to go back to Santiago as fast as possible."

"We don't want to let Santana's trail grow cold," Joe added.

Soon afterward, the Hardys were on the road again. They reached Santiago, turned their car in at the renting office, and walked to South American Antiquities. Bertrand was in his office inspecting some Incan artifacts.

"Did you catch Santana?" he asked eagerly.

"We caught up with him," Frank replied. "But he got away again."

Bertrand stared at them in disappointment when they explained what happened.

"Well, that leaves me no choice," the antique dealer said finally. "I'll have to call the police."

"Mr. Kimberley didn't want that," Joe objected. "Why don't you give us another chance to look for Santana in Santiago?"

Bertrand was doubtful. "I'll let you know tomorrow morning," he said with a sigh. "It's late now, and I want to go home." Wearily, he escorted the Hardys to the door.

The boys discussed the case in their hotel room that night. "All we have to go on is a name— Ernesto," Joe said.

Frank nodded. "We might be better off asking the police for help, as Bertrand suggested," he said.

"Kimberley didn't want the authorities involved, but that was because he signed the release for the idol and would have been the prime suspect. Now we know he didn't take it. And the police might have some idea who Ernesto is, or even have a record of Santana!"

"You're right," Joe admitted. "Let's—"

Just then the telephone rang. Frank answered, and his face broke into a smile. "Hi, Dad," he said. "What's happening?"

"You tell me first," Fenton Hardy replied, and the young detective explained their adventures in the Easter Island idol case.

"You did fine work," his father commended him. "But as far as Santana is concerned, I'm afraid you'll have to let the police handle him."

"We were thinking of asking the authorities for help," Frank admitted. "But we want to keep searching for him, too. We have the Ernesto clue."

"I know," his father said. "But I'd like you to put the case on the back burner and help me for a while."

"Why, Dad? Do you need us?"

"I do. I'd like you to leave Santiago as soon as possible."

"Where are we going?"

"The Antarctic!"

8 A New Plan

Frank and Joe stared at one another. They could hear their father chuckling over the phone.

"I thought that would interest you," the detective said. "I can't tell you any details at this point. Just catch a flight to Punta Arenas. It's in Tierra del Fuego at the southern tip of South America. Belongs to Chile. There's a plane out of Santiago tomorrow. I've already made reservations for you."

"What do we do after we land?" Frank wanted to know.

"You'll find out when you get there. An advisor will meet you at the information booth. I have to go now. Bye." With that, Fenton Hardy hung up.

"Dad's really being mysterious," Frank observed. "I wonder where he is."

"Probably in Washington," Joe said. "Anyway, we won't be going back to New York for a while. What do you say we call Kimberley?"

"Good idea. He must be wondering if we've found the idol. But it's too late now. Let's do it in the morning."

After breakfast the following day, Joe phoned South American Antiquities in New York.

"What have you found out?" Kimberley demanded. "Any progress to report?"

"That strange message you gave us was a clue," Joe responded. "It showed us where to look for the idol—in a secret compartment."

"Oh?"

"Behind a photo of the Andes in the outer office of your Santiago branch. A small panel slid back when we lifted the photo off the wall. The peg worked as an automatic control."

"I've seen that compartment!" Kimberley thundered. "It was there when we rented the office."

"I know," Joe said. "Mr. Bertrand told us most of the staff were aware of its existence."

"But what about the idol. Was it there?"

"It sure was. We were about to take it out when your chauffeur ran up to us and grabbed it."

"Julio? Are you talking about Julio Santana?"

"Yes, sir."

There was silence on the other end of the line.

Finally Kimberley spoke again. "I can't imagine that Julio is a thief. Do you know if—if he was the one who put the idol there in the first place?"

"No. But he *could* have done it," Joe said. "Mr. Bertrand left to get ice when you were picking up your watch that night in the Santiago hotel. Santana could have sneaked into the room and removed the sculpture from your case with a duplicate key."

"That must be it, then," Kimberley said. "Where's Santana now, in jail?"

"No," Joe replied and reported what had happened in the mountain village.

Kimberley grunted. "You let him escape? What kind of detectives are you? I'm going to ask my partner to call the police!"

"We wanted to suggest the same thing, sir," Frank said evenly. "Our father needs us to help him on his case and we have to interrupt our activities here temporarily."

"Temporarily!" Kimberley sneered. "By the time you come back, I hope Santana will have been caught!"

"So do we," Frank said politely.

After the conversation ended, Frank spoke with Bertrand and explained that he and Joe were leaving Santiago to help their father.

"We'll return as soon as we can to help find the idol if the police aren't successful," he promised.

"Okay," Bertrand said. "I'll call the chief and tell him the whole story."

The Hardys packed their things, checked out of the hotel, and left for the airport. Suddenly, Frank had an idea. "We're headed for Punta Arenas," he said. "That's where Santana once worked in the oil fields. Maybe he's planning to go back there, take his old job, and lie low until the heat's off and he can sell the idol!"

"He might even be on the same plane as we are," Joe added excitedly. "He and the other fellow!"

At the terminal, the brothers boarded their flight and took their seats. Holding magazines before their faces to conceal themselves, they pretended to read while furtively watching the passengers coming aboard. But they saw only strangers.

The plane took off on a flight that lasted several hours. Finally Punta Arenas came into view. The Hardys could see oil rigs spotted around the oil fields. Incandescent flames flared atop tall towers and showed where superfluous gas was being burned off. Trucks were carrying barrels of oil down toward the port where tankers waited at anchor for their cargo.

The plane landed at the airport outside the city, and the Hardys filed out with the other passengers.

"I wonder who the advisor is who's meeting us here," Frank commented.

"Since we don't know, he'd better recognize *us,*" Joe chuckled.

They entered the terminal, collected their suitcases, and walked to the information booth, waiting expectantly for their contact to arrive.

Suddenly they heard a familiar voice behind them. "Hi, boys!"

Whirling around, they saw Fenton Hardy!

"Dad, you're the advisor we're supposed to meet!" Joe exclaimed.

"What are you doing here?" Frank inquired. "We thought you were in Washington."

"It's a long story. I'll tell you during our flight to Antarctica. We'll be boarding a U.S. Navy plane in a few minutes. It's standing by on one of the runways. You see, the American and Chilean governments cooperate in the air transport from here to bases near the South Pole."

Joe mentioned that Santana had once worked in the Punta Arenas oil fields. "He might be headed this way again."

"No time for that right now," Fenton Hardy declared. "But I'll alert the authorities."

He went to a phone, talked briefly, and returned. "The company Santana worked for has his name in its inoperative files. The police will get in touch with the personnel department in case he tries to get his job back."

An American naval officer approached and said, "Mr. Hardy, we're ready for takeoff."

"Thank you." The detective led the way to the plane, which bore on its side the legend: U.S. NAVY ANTARCTIC EXPLORATION. The Hardys found themselves among naval personnel and scientists who specialized in research in the area.

"It's safe to talk now," Fenton Hardy said as the flight began. "You boys already know that I'm investigating the theft of government materiel from some of our naval bases. I found that a big ring has been operating, and identified the small-fry. They'll be arrested. But I'm up against a stone wall with regard to one gang member."

"The ringleader?" Frank asked.

Fenton Hardy nodded. "My investigation indicates that he's one of the crew at Byrd Base, our newest Antarctic installation. But I have no idea who he is."

"So the navy wants you to go down there and find out."

"Exactly. I've had to be hush-hush about the case because the ringleader may have spies at Punta Arenas. I don't want them to tip him off. There are one hundred men at Byrd Base, so it won't be easy to identify the culprit. My cover story is that I'm a scientist reporting on the laboratories they're using."

"And what about us?" Joe inquired.

"I have a special assignment for you. There's a small advance installation beyond Byrd Base. It's called Outpost I. The gang chief might be there, so I want you to investigate."

"We'll need a cover story, too," Frank pointed out. "We can't just go barging in and say we're the Hardys boys looking for a thief!"

"That's been taken care of," his father assured him. "Two students who won scholarships for Antarctic training have been withdrawn from Outpost I. Your cover story is that you're replacing them temporarily. You've got enough science from Bayport High to fit in without any trouble."

"Just think—investigating at the South Pole!" Joe exclaimed. "We've never done that before!"

Fenton Hardy smiled at his son's enthusiasm. Then he became serious again. "Just remember," he said, "we're going to one of the toughest spots on the globe. Besides being cold, it'll be extremely dangerous!"

9 *Penguin Attack*

Fenton Hardy took a map of the Antarctic and spread it out on his knees.

"You can see that the continent around the South Pole lies almost entirely within the Antarctic Circle," he said to Frank and Joe. "The main exception is the Antarctic Peninsula pushing in the direction of Tierra del Fuego. These two large indentations of the coastline are caused by the Weddell Sea below the Antarctic Peninsula and the Ross Sea on the opposite side of the continent."

"Is Byrd Base near Little America?" Frank asked.

"It's about two hundred miles up the coast, on the Ross Shelf, which connects the Ross Sea and the

Antarctic Continent. We'll be on the continent itself. No neighbors near Byrd Base. A lot of nations have installations in the Antarctic. But it's a big place."

"And it's peaceful," Joe commented. "We learned that when we were studying about the International Geophysical Year in school. All the nations agreed not to fight over claims in the Antarctic."

The three Hardys began discussing the heroic days of exploration in the area, especially the race to the South Pole between Roald Amundsen of Norway and Robert Scott of Great Britain.

"Amundsen reached the pole first," Frank said. "That was in 1911, before the days of radio communication, and Scott knew nothing about it until he and his men got to the South Pole and found Amundsen's flag flying over it."

"Then the members of the Scott expedition were lost in a desperate trek back from the pole," Joe added. "Later, their bodies were found by a rescue team. Scott's diary tells the story."

"And of course you know about Admiral Richard E. Byrd, who established Little America and pioneered the use of airplanes in the Antarctic," Mr. Hardy spoke up. "Byrd and another pilot, Bernt Balchen, were the first to fly over the South Pole."

"We could go on forever talking about Antarctic

exploration," Frank said. "But I think I'll catch a little shuteye."

"Good idea," Joe agreed. "I'm bushed myself from all this traveling." He leaned back in his seat and soon all were asleep.

When they woke up, they looked out the window at the cold gray billows of the Polar Sea. An icebreaker, which seemed like a toy ship far below, was slowly cutting a path through ice several feet thick.

The plane crossed the water and land appeared. Tall, windswept mountains came into view. From their foothills, a grim wasteland of ice and snow broken by glaciers extended into the distance.

"Looks pretty desolate out there," Frank said.

Just then, the pilot came down the aisle and stopped in front of the boys. "I'm Captain Roeloffs," he introduced himself. "I understand you boys are student scientists. Perhaps you'd like to come into the cockpit and see what the Antarctic is like from there."

"We sure would," Frank and Joe said at once.

"Follow me, then," the pilot said. He led the way up the aisle into the cockpit. The copilot grinned a greeting as the Hardys slipped into the two seats behind him. Roeloffs sat down in his chair. "We're on automatic pilot," he said, "and we'll stay that way until we reach the South Pole."

Frank was studying a map of the Antarctic. "If we fly to the pole, won't it be to the left of the Ross Ice Shelf? Won't we miss Byrd Base?"

"We're dropping supplies to the Amundsen-Scott Station at the pole," the pilot explained. "After that, we'll turn right to Byrd Base."

The plane thundered on over a bleak landscape, and the Hardys could see directly ahead to the Transantarctic Mountains, a long chain of rugged peaks extending from one side of the continent to the other. As they crossed the mountains, deep valleys and enormous glaciers came into view.

"Want to go backpacking down there?" Frank kidded his brother.

"It would be too easy," Joe quipped. "I like the real outdoors, like the Bayport Woods!"

Some huts became visible, and men emerged running toward the plane and waving their arms.

"Boys," Roeloffs said as he switched off the automatic control and began to fly the craft himself, "we're now at the South Pole!"

"Looks just like the rest of the snow," Frank observed.

"We don't need a compass now," Joe commented. "From here, every direction is north."

The plane circled over the Amundsen–Scott Station. Crates of supplies went out the cargo door, plummeted toward the snow, and pulled up sharply as their parachutes opened. They drifted down to where the men from the huts were waiting to pick them up.

The copilot, who had been talking to the station by radio, said a farewell. Then the plane turned away from the pole and headed for the Ross Ice Shelf.

When they arrived, Roeloffs cut the power and the plane landed on a frozen runway at Byrd Base.

The passengers filed out in the direction of a two-story building with wings extending to the rear on either side. It was made of prefabricated boards attached to a steel frame. A helicopter equipped with skis stood near a number of Antarctic vehicles such as motor toboggans and Sno-Cats.

About twenty men were handling the vehicles, conducting weather experiments, or collecting samples of ice and snow. They wore heavy clothing and waved at the new arrivals, who hurried in out of the frigid cold. The commander of Byrd Base greeted them in the main room. He held a list of names in his hand.

"I'm Admiral Ian Langton," he announced. "If you'll gather around, I'll tell you what your assignments are."

"We'll stay out of this," Fenton Hardy said to his sons in an undertone. "We're on a secret mission, so we'll talk to the admiral later."

The other men received their instructions and left to settle in and get to work. When the last one had disappeared, the Bayport sleuth introduced himself and the boys.

"I'm glad to see you," Langton said. "Come to my office and we'll discuss your mission. All I know is that the navy's keeping it under wraps."

In the office, Fenton Hardy described his discovery of a gang of thieves operating at American naval bases. "Clues indicate that the ringleader is here at Byrd Base," he explained. "My assignment is to find out who he is. Frank and Joe will help with the investigation."

The admiral shook his head. "It's hard for me to believe the ringleader is one of my men. But of course we've only been here a short time. I don't know all of them yet. Anyway, I received orders from the navy to bring a couple of student scientists back from Outpost I. I suppose you can tell me why."

"The man we're looking for might be at Outpost I," Fenton Hardy replied. "Frank and Joe will replace the students. I will stay here at Byrd Base in the guise of a scientist assigned to see how the labs are working."

"Since you three are using science as a cover story," Langton said, "I'd better introduce you to my scientific advisor, Professor Sigmund Muller. Come with me."

The admiral led the way to an office where a desk was piled high with reports and documents. Muller sat in a chair behind the desk writing in a notebook. He had gray hair and wore steel-rimmed glasses. Langton introduced the Hardys, and he gave them a warm greeting. The admiral then explained the secret mission that had brought them to Byrd Base.

"Oh, no!" Muller exclaimed. "How could the ringleader of a gang of thieves be among us?"

"I only got on to him by a process of elimination," Fenton Hardy explained. "I found it hard to believe he would operate out of the Antarctic. But every other possibility failed, which means he must be stationed at Byrd Base or Outpost 1."

"If that's the case, I'm glad you're here," said Muller in a hearty tone. "I'll pretend you're new members of my scientific team."

"Sigmund, why don't you show Frank and Joe around?" Langton suggested.

"I'll be glad to," Muller agreed as the admiral and Fenton Hardy returned to Langton's office. Muller took the boys into one wing of the building, which housed the science department of the base.

In the first laboratory, a number of long columns

of frozen earth were laid out on a table side by side. Several men were working on them.

"These are core samples from the crust of the Antarctic Continent," Muller explained. "They tell us about the age of the Antarctic. We know it's been here for many millions of years."

In other laboratories, scientists were carrying out experiments in physics and chemistry. An aquarium held fish from the Antarctic Sea. Storerooms oocupied the end of the wing. They were filled with scientific instruments, samples of earth and rock, and stuffed birds, seals, and fish.

Muller introduced Frank and Joe to the staff as they moved from one room to another. The Hardys kept their eyes open for clues, but saw nothing to indicate that a crook was hiding at Byrd Base.

Finally Muller pointed to piles of heavy clothing on the shelves of a storeroom. "Now you'd better get into these," he said. "We're going outside."

"I don't see any furs," Joe commented as they dressed.

Their host laughed. "People wore furs back in the days of Admiral Byrd. Today we have special clothing designed by navy experts. You'll find those parkas as warm as a sealskin coat, and much lighter and more comfortable."

Pulling the hoods of their jackets over their heads, the three emerged from the building. A cold wind blew in their faces and momentarily took their breath away.

A meteorologist atop a steel scaffolding was knocking ice off a weathervane to allow the instrument to move freely in the wind. Other workers were releasing a weather balloon, which drifted upward, blowing wildly to and fro.

"The balloon is filled with helium," the leader of the group explained. "It'll reach the upper atmosphere and tell us how the winds blow around the South Pole. The temperature sometimes hits one hundred below zero."

After some discussion of the cons during which the Antarctic turned from a warm area into a frigid wilderness, Muller conducted the Hardys on a walk through the snow down to the shore. They stopped at a point where a cliff dipped in rugged contours into water filled with ice floes.

On one side, the terrain rose and fell in a series of low hills. On the other side, it stretched out in a level plain where the Hardys could see moving black patches against the white background of the ice.

"Penguins!" Frank and Joe exclaimed in unison.

"Come on for a closer look," Muller invited.

The three walked down into the penguin rookery. It contained hundreds of the black and white Antarctic birds. Some were roosting on the ice, others waddled around in an upright position, still others dived into the water.

The waddling birds made the Hardys laugh. Joe pointed to a penguin about three feet tall advancing toward them. Its color pattern gave it the appearance of wearing a white shirt and black coat. It moved in a shuffling walk.

"That one's as funny as a clown at the circus," Joe commented. "I think I'll take a picture of it."

He pulled his miniature camera out of his pocket. Moving forward, he dropped to one knee and started to focus on the approaching bird.

Suddenly the penguin thrust its neck forward and opened its beak menacingly. It rushed forward with an angry cackle, and Joe began to retreat. Just then he slipped on the ice and lost his footing, falling right in the angry penguin's path!

10 The Sno-Cat

The penguin snapped at Joe with its beak and flailed
at him with its stubby wings before he could finally
scramble clear and retreat.

"Saved by the bell!" Frank laughed. "Want to go a
few more rounds with the champ, Joe?"

The younger Hardy boy gingerly tested a sore
spot on his nose where the penguin had nipped
him. "No thanks!" he groaned. "I'm hanging up the
gloves after this one. What got into that critter
anyway, Professor?"

Muller chuckled. "They're usually tame, Joe.
This one must be an exception."

"That penguin got up on the wrong side of the
nest this morning," Frank quipped, "and he just
didn't want to have his picture taken."

"Let's look at the Antarctic vehicles," Muller suggested.

The three walked over to the helicopter. The Hardys noted it was just like the choppers they had flown at Bayport airfield except for the skis.

"That's the way to travel down here," Frank said. "No mushing over the snow."

Muller nodded but cautioned, "If you boys ever go up, look out for the wind. You might get blown off course."

"We'll watch out," Joe promised. "Who wants to crash-land at the South Pole?"

"Anyway, we do most of our traveling in these vehicles," Muller continued. He pointed to the machines standing near the helicopter. "Motor toboggans and Sno-Cats."

The toboggans were long, narrow vehicles, open on all sides but protected from the Antarctic blast by a windshield mounted on the front. They were propelled by a motor connected to revolving chains with cleats on either side. The cleats biting into the ice diminished the danger that the chains would spin instead of moving the toboggan.

The Sno-Cats looked like trucks for hauling heavy cargo except that the four wheels were replaced by tractor treads.

"This is the workhorse of the Antarctic," Muller commented. "It has four-wheel drive—or I should say, four-tread drive. Each tread can be operated independently, enabling the driver to maneuver over rocky terrain, through deep snow, and past crevasses where one tread may be hanging over the edge. Well, now you've seen all our equipment. We might as well go in."

The pleasant aroma of cooking wafted from the galley as they entered, and the chef beat on a small, copper gong.

"Chow time!" he called out.

The scientists and naval personnel began streaming into the dining room where long wooden tables were laid with dishes and cutlery. The men sat on makeshift benches made of planks nailed to crossbars extending from the tables at each end.

The Hardys found themselves sitting next to a youth about their own age.

"I'm Bob Field," he introduced himself. "I'm a freshman with a scholarship in geology, so I'm spending a year at Byrd Base. Actually, I was at Outpost I, but they ordered me and another student to come back here."

Frank and Joe questioned him about his work at Outpost I.

"How long were you there?" Frank asked. "My brother Joe and I find it pretty bleak in this icy desert. I bet after a while it gets to you."

"It does," Bob admitted. "But the work's extremely interesting. I've been doing research on core samples. We're using the uranium method."

"We're familiar with that," Frank said. "All rocks contain uranium, which turns into lead at a very slow, steady pace."

"And the amount of uranium in relation to the amount of lead gives you a fix on the age of the sample," Joe added.

The three continued a lively discussion of Antarctic rocks. Then Frank asked Bob if he did anything else at the base.

"Part-time radioman," was the reply.

"What kind of messages do you send? High-level technical information?"

"No. Just routine stuff—reports to navy ships in the Ross Sea, weather warnings to other Antarctic bases, things like that."

"Could we watch you work sometime?"

"Oh, I'm sure it wouldn't interest you."

After the meal was over, the Hardys went to a corner of the lounge to discuss the situation.

"What did Bob mean by saying we wouldn't be interested in his radio messages?" Joe wondered. "He sounded to me like he was afraid we might discover something."

"Could be," Frank responded. "As a radioman, he would be in a position to communicate with gang members on other bases. We'd better keep an eye on him."

"He could hardly be the ringleader, though," Joe said. "I would think it takes more than a college freshman to run a gang of thieves spread out all over the world."

Fenton Hardy joined them, and they reported to him their suspicion of Bob Field.

"I'll keep an eye on him," their father promised. "You boys will be pushing off for Outpost I tomorrow. Any delay would look suspicious. Report to Professor Muller in the morning."

"Dad, have you spotted any clues?" Joe asked.

Fenton Hardy shook his head. "Nothing yet. But I'll keep checking while you two are investigating at Outpost I. I don't want to go into it now because we shouldn't be seen with our heads together too much. The ringleader of the gang might figure out what we're up to."

He rose to his feet and walked off. Frank and Joe picked a couple of books from the library shelves and read until it was time to turn in with the rest of the men. They all slept in one room, where each had a locker at the foot of the bed and hooks on the wall to hang clothes.

Bob Field had a bed next to the Hardys. As he was hanging up his shirt, Joe noticed a piece of paper in the breast pocket. The sheet was fine enough for Joe to see the word "radiogram" in reverse on the other side.

"That could be a message Bob's sending for the ringleader!" the boy thought excitedly. "I'd better have a look at it."

Joe waited until Bob and the rest were sound asleep, then he silently slipped out of his bed. He retrieved a pencil flashlight from his jacket pocket, stealthily edged over to Bob's clothes, and eased the paper out of the breast pocket of the shirt. Slowly and carefully, to avoid making any noise, he opened the paper and played the beam of his flashlight on it.

The message was:

TO SUPPLY SHIP *BALCHEN.* REQUEST MORE CANNED PEAS. STORES RUNNING LOW. SIGNED IAN LANGTON, ADMIRAL, USN.

Grinning in the darkness, Joe pushed the paper back into Bob's shirt pocket. He doused his flashlight, returned to his bed, and fell asleep.

In the morning, he took the first opportunity to tell Frank about the night's episode.

"Great detective work!" Frank laughed. "You set out to expose a crook and ended up with an order for canned peas!"

Joe nodded sheepishly. "Well, let's see if anything is cooking in the admiral's quarters."

The boys left the dormitory and found their father with Langton.

"I don't have a break in the case yet," Fenton Hardy told them. "You two go to Outpost I. We can communicate by radio if anything develops."

"How do we get there?" Frank inquired.

"By Sno-Cat," Langton replied. "You'll be traveling by yourselves because the route's quite easy to follow. Now, report to Professor Muller. He'll explain the details."

Frank and Joe walked down the corridor to Muller's office. The scientific advisor was shuffling papers on his desk.

"Here's what you need to get to Outpost I safely," he said and pulled a map out of his desk drawer. "This will show you where Outpost I is located."

He took a pen and made a cross on the map. "Go directly toward the inland mountain with two peaks," Muller advised, "then you stop at the large glacier at the base of the mountain. Turn west, go twenty miles, and you'll see the outpost on a broad plain of ice and snow."

He handed the map to Frank. "It really isn't very far and it's easy to find."

"What's it like?" Joe queried.

"It's made up of two small, wooden buildings.

You'll see an American flag flying from a pole out front. I'll have our radioman send them a message to expect you. All that remains now is your transportation. Come on outside."

The Hardys' Sno-Cat was ready. Antarctic clothing for them had been stowed in a compartment opposite the steering wheel, and the back of the vehicle was filled with crates of food. More provisions were lashed to a heavy sled tied to the rear of the Sno-Cat by a stout rope.

"These are supplies for the outpost," Muller explained. "You're to deliver them to Commander Noonan, who's in charge. Then you'll join the crew as student scientists and see if you can break the case you're on."

"We'd like to say good-bye to our father," Frank said.

"Sure," Muller said. "He's probably in the admiral's office. Go on inside. You can leave your things out here."

The boys put their overnight bags in the Sno-Cat and laid the map on the dashboard. Then they went to see the admiral and Mr. Hardy.

"Good luck, boys," the investigator said. "Make notes on everything that you find suspicious. I'll contact you later and we'll talk about it."

"Sure thing, Dad," Frank said and the boys shook hands with the two men. Then they went outside again and climbed into the Sno-Cat, waving to a few crew members who were watching them.

Frank started the motor. The treads of the vehicle began turning, and the rope grew taut in the rear as the heavy sled started to move.

"Here we go into the wilderness," Joe said with a wry grin. "Left out in the cold, so to speak."

"What I'd like to know," his brother said, squinting his eyes against the whiteness around him, "is—will we find what we're looking for?"

11 Lost in the Antarctic

The Sno-Cat clanked forward over the ice and the powdery snow. Occasionally, the treads ground over outcroppings of rock with a harsh, metallic sound. An hour passed.

"The motor's purring like a kitten," Frank observed.

"Good thing, Frank. If we stall, it's a long walk back to Byrd Base!"

Joe took a pair of binoculars from the glove compartment and focused on the terrain up ahead. "I see the mountain with the two peaks," he announced. Measuring the angle with his compass, he added, "Two degrees to the left, Frank, and you'll be on the beam."

"Okay."

Soon, they could see the mountain with their naked eyes. It rose like a solitary sentinel in the distance. There was no sign of life anywhere, no animals on the ground or birds in the sky.

"It's eerie out here," Joe commented as he gazed at the wilderness. A snowstorm was approaching.

"At least there's no parking problem," Frank joked.

The Sno-Cat rumbled forward through howling wind and falling snow. Hitting a slippery patch of ice, Frank had to use his four-wheel drive as first one tread and then another began to spin because it could not get a grip on the ice.

The Hardys crossed this slippery area and kept going until they reached the mountain. There Frank brought the Sno-Cat to a halt.

"Joe, do you see the glacier?" he asked.

Joe shook his head. "It must be on the other side. Let's see."

Starting the engine again, Frank drove around the base of the mountain. They strained their eyes to see if they could make out the glacier through the wind and snow.

Suddenly they felt the Sno-Cat moving sideways!

"We're *on* the glacier!" Frank shouted.

Desperately, he threw the vehicle into reverse. The moving river of ice caught it and spun it in a semicircle. They swung toward the end of the glacier where a tumbled mass of ice blocks threatened to crush them!

At the last moment, helped by the weight of the sled behind, the left rear tread caught on solid terrain. Frank quickly flipped the switch that fed all the power to that tread, and the Sno-Cat moved backward, pushing the sled as it went. Then the right rear tread gripped the ground. This permitted the vehicle to back all the way off the glacier.

Frank wiped perspiration from his brow. "Wow!" he gasped. "That's the first time I ever drove sideways!"

Joe chuckled, trying to overcome the fear he had felt only seconds before. "You just won your Sno-Cat driver's license."

"Anyway, we found the glacier, and are on the last leg of this trip."

"Right," Joe said. "Now go west for twenty miles."

He took a compass reading, and they clanked forward over hills and down into valleys. Checking his instruments, Frank counted off the miles.

"Twenty!" he said at last.

"We should reach Outpost I at any moment," Joe said, again resorting to the binoculars for a better view ahead. However, all he could see was endless ice and snow.

They rolled on and on, and the snow stopped falling. Now the terrain became more level.

After a while, Frank spoke up. "Maybe we bypassed the place. We could have missed it in the snowstorm. See if you can raise them on the radio, Joe. They can guide us in."

Joe took the receiver from the dashboard and flicked the "on" button. However, no sound came from the instrument! He banged it with the heel of his hand, but to no avail. Then he opened the back to check the batteries. The case was empty!

"No batteries!" Joe groaned. "How did that happen?" He quickly searched the cabin for spares, but there were none. "The guy who fixed the Sno-Cat for us must have forgotten them. What a mistake!"

"Let's look at the map Muller gave us," Frank suggested. "Maybe we made a mistake, too."

Joe picked up the map and unfolded it. Then he gasped. "The cross Muller made to indicate the outpost's location isn't there!" he cried out.

"What!" Frank stopped the Sno-Cat and stared at the map.

"Someone must have changed maps on us," Joe said. "While we were inside saying good-bye to Dad and Admiral Langton."

"Same guy who swiped the radio batteries," Frank added. "It figures."

"No, it doesn't," Joe insisted. "I remember Muller said to turn west at the glacier, and that's what we did!"

"Are you sure he didn't say east?"

"Yes—well—I thought he said west."

Frank pointed to a small hill to the right. "Let's climb up there and take our bearings. I'll maneuver as close as I can get."

He drove forward toward the hill. Suddenly, the snow gave way under the right front tread! He cut the engine instantly, but the Sno-Cat tilted up on end and the tread hung over empty air! The Hardys stared down into an icy crevasse hundreds of feet deep!

They shivered as they realized that any movement might cause the vehicle to lose its balance and topple over the edge, hurtling them to the bottom of the crevasse!

"We can't take a chance and climb out," Frank muttered. "I'll have to see if I can drive us out of this corner. Keep your fingers crossed, Joe!"

Carefully, he turned on the motor and put the vehicle into reverse. It teetered on the edge of the crevasse while the Hardys held their breath. Then the two treads still on firm snow took hold and rolled the Sno-Cat to a point where gravity took over and dragged the vehicle onto its third tread.

The fourth still hung over the crevasse, but Frank was now able to drive back and let it regain its normal position.

He mopped his forehead with a handkerchief. "We're driving an obstacle course!" he groaned. "This is very dangerous!"

"I know," Joe said grimly. "Well, we're close enough to walk to the top of the hill. Let's hope we can spot Outpost I from there."

He took the heavy Antarctic clothing from the compartment behind them. They donned thick leather boots, rough trousers, parkas, and fur gloves. Pulling goggles over their eyes, they emerged from the Sno-Cat into a high wind.

They roped themselves together. Using alpenstocks—wooden staffs with metal tips—to help them keep their footing, they set out for the hill with Frank in the lead.

At every step, they tested the snow with their alpenstocks to make sure it was strong enough to support them. Skirting past the crevasse into which they had nearly fallen, they tramped along under a sky the dismal color of lead. The sun was barely discernible over their heads, and the only sound they could hear was the wind and their own footsteps.

Reaching the bottom of the hill, the Hardys

began to climb it step by step, sometimes over snow and ice, sometimes over the frozen earth and rock of the Antarctic. They gasped in the frigid air.

About halfway up, they came to a rocky ledge, where they stopped for a rest, discussing their predicament.

"Unless we took the wrong turn, Outpost I has to be in sight from the top of the hill!" Frank declared. "Even if we bypassed it in the storm, we can't have missed it by much."

"Right," Joe said. He made sure the rope connecting them was securely tied before they resumed their climb. It was a difficult ascent because they had to feel with their alpenstocks for places where they could get safe toeholds. The cold wind blowing in their faces made them lean into it in order to maintain their balance.

As they rounded a rocky wall, Frank stepped onto an icy cliff. At the same time, a violent gust made him stagger to one side. He slipped and skidded along the ice toward the side of the cliff, dragging Joe after him!

Then, finding nothing to break his momentum, he went right over the edge!

Suddenly Joe came to a bone-crunching halt as his boot soles slammed against an outcropping of rock protruding from the ice. The rope around his

waist tightened as it stopped Frank's fall down the face of the cliff!

"Frank, hang on!" Joe yelled.

"I've got my foot on a rock sticking out of the side," Frank called back. "I can climb up if you help me."

"Will do!"

Joe yanked on the rope with all his might. He played it in, hand over hand, so Frank could brace his feet against the side of the cliff and work his way back to the ledge. Then both sat down gasping for breath.

"It's good we're tied together, or I'd been at the bottom of the cliff," Frank muttered.

Joe peered over the edge. "Well, our alpenstocks are down there. I can see them lying in the snow."

"They'll stay there, Joe. I'm not about to go and get them!"

"Neither am I. Let's make tracks up the hill, okay?"

Getting to their feet, they again climbed toward the top. They moved more slowly and carefully than before because they no longer had their alpenstocks with which to feel for the safest path upward. Finally the slant of the hill became less steep, and they struggled to the summit.

Planting their feet firmly and bracing themselves against the wind, the Hardys surveyed the terrain all around them. They saw an expanse of ice and snow extending to the horizon in every direction except to the west, where a range of mountains cut the skyline in a series of tall peaks. No buildings, no flagpole, broke the uniformity of the white landscape.

The Hardys stared at one another in dismay as the meaning became clear to them.

"We're lost!" Joe exclaimed. "We might never find our way out of here!"

12 Two Suspects

Joe took the binoculars and looked around. He saw only ice, snow, and mountains. "What do we do now?" he wondered.

The wind was becoming stronger and colder, and the boys struggled to keep their feet on the hilltop. Shivering, they pulled their parka hoods across their faces for protection.

"Let's go back to the Sno-Cat," Frank said. "At least it's warm."

They made their way down the hill, which was easier than climbing up. Carefully they inched along the icy ledge where Frank had fallen, circled past the crevasse that threatened them, and got into the Sno-Cat, where they removed their Antarctic gear.

"There's no use continuing west," Joe pointed out. "We'd only end up in the mountains. Anyway, Outpost I isn't out there."

"We don't have enough gas to get back to Byrd Base," Frank observed. "And we sure don't want to get stranded. But if west isn't the right direction, then Muller must have said east."

"Right," Joe said. "Unless he sent us in the wrong direction deliberately, hoping our Sno-Cat would fall into the crevasse and we'd never be found!"

"He could have exchanged the map while we were talking to Dad and the admiral. This way there would be no proof," Frank added grimly.

Joe nodded. "And he might have snitched the batteries so we couldn't contact anyone."

Frank started the engine, and they drove back along the route they had taken. Spotting the mountain with the two peaks, they reached the glacier where the Sno-Cat had nearly been swept away. Twenty miles of travel beyond that point over the frozen terrain brought them within view of a tall flagpole flying the stars and stripes. Two small wooden buildings stood nearby, one bearing a sign reading: U.S. NAVY OUTPOST I.

"Boy, am I glad we made it!" Frank said, looking at the gas gauge. "We couldn't have gone much farther!"

Seven men were working with polar equipment

in front of the installation. One of them came up as Frank stopped the Sno-Cat and the Hardys got out.

"I'm Commander Noonan," he said. "Welcome to Outpost I. You must be the Hardy boys."

Frank and Joe shook hands with Noonan, but did not tell him that they almost had not made it.

"We'd like to radio Byrd Base and tell our father that we've arrived," Frank said instead.

"Sure thing," Noonan replied. "I'll have my radioman show you the equipment. He'll be here in a moment. Meanwhile, let me introduce you to my crew."

The men were scientists working on the geology and meteorology of the Antarctic.

"Stones and storms," Joe quipped.

"That's our subject." Noonan laughed. "We're big on weather reports."

An eighth man emerged from one of the buildings. He was short and thin. He glanced around uneasily as he walked up to the group.

"Al Ambrose, meet Frank and Joe Hardy." Noonan introduced them. "Al's our radioman."

Ambrose looked at the Hardys in astonishment. His eyes widened and his mouth fell open. However, with some effort he managed to regain his composure.

"He's worried about something," Joe thought. "And he's not glad to see us."

Noonan ordered Ambrose to show the Hardys to the living quarters of Outpost I. "Then take them to the radio shack. They want to send a message to Byrd Base."

"Impossible, sir," Ambrose replied quickly. "The radio's out. I'm trying to find the bug in the equipment."

"Well, let them know as soon as you have it fixed. Now, the three of you better go in."

The radioman conducted the Hardys into one of the buildings. "This is our living quarters," he informed them. "The other structure is for the technical work. I've got my radio shack over there."

A corridor led from the door to the rear of the building. Flanking the hallway at the front were a number of storerooms on either side. Then came the kitchen facing the dining room and living room, followed by an infirmary and a small gym complete with exercycle.

At the end of the corridor, the dormitory occupied most of the width of the building. Ten cots stood in two rows along the walls. The remaining space was taken up by the private room of the commander.

Ambrose pointed to the two cots nearest the doorway. "These are yours," he told the Hardys. "They belonged to the two students who went back to Byrd Base."

Frank thanked him, then asked in a friendly tone, "What do you think's wrong with your radio, Al?"

"Search me," the young man replied. "I'm trying to find out."

"Need any help? We've had a lot of experience in that field."

"That's all right. I'll handle it myself."

"He doesn't want us to see his equipment," Joe thought. Aloud he said, "Where do you come from in the States?"

"San Diego."

"There's a big naval base in San Diego."

"One of the biggest. Well, you guys are on your own now. I'm going to work on the radio. Tell you when I have it operational." With that, Al left whistling a tune off-key.

Frank looked at Joe. "I bet Muller tipped Ambrose off about the scheme to have us disappear! That's why Al was so surprised to see us. He was hoping we'd be at the bottom of that crevasse way off in the west near the mountains!"

"That means his radio was working earlier today," Joe continued his brother's thought. "I think he's only pretending it's on the blink. Let's sneak into the shack when he's not around and raise Byrd Base!"

"He might put the radio out of commission deliberately, Joe."

"I know. But it's worth a try."

The Hardys went outside to help unload the Sno-Cat and the sled. The crates and boxes were carried into the building and stacked in the store-rooms.

By now it was getting dark, and the crew congregated in the living quarters. Ambrose, who doubled as a cook, was heading for the kitchen.

He stopped near the Hardys and said, "The vacuum tubes are gone and there are none in stock. We'll have to wait for Byrd Base to send technical supplies."

"Well, help should be on the way soon," Frank declared. "They probably know by now that our radio is out."

"Let's hope so," Ambrose mumbled and disappeared into the kitchen. While the radioman whipped up a spicy goulash, Frank made his way to the radio shack to check Al's story. He found the sender inoperable as Ambrose had told them, and quickly returned to the living room.

"It's out all right," he reported to Joe. "But I don't know whether it was done deliberately or not."

When the meal was ready, the men filed past a counter at the kitchen door, where Al, wielding a large ladle, filled their plates. Then they entered the dining room, which was just large enough to hold a round table and ten chairs.

Ambrose came in and sat between Frank and Joe.

"This is great goulash," Joe said as he downed a mouthful.

"A bit too hot for me," Frank muttered and took a long drink of water.

"The other guys like it hot," Ambrose explained.

After dinner, the three went into the dorm and talked for a while about the rigors of life in the Antarctic. Frank stretched and yawned. "I think I'll hit the hay," he declared. "I'm bushed."

"It's bedtime for us all," Ambrose stated. "We get up early here, and we need all the sleep we can get."

Frank crawled into his cot and fell sound asleep. One by one the others turned in. Joe noticed Ambrose snap out the overhead light just before he dozed off.

He was awakened in the middle of the night by a hand shaking him. A voice whispered into his ear, "Joe, this is Al Ambrose. Commander Noonan wants to see you. Frank's with him now and he says it's important. Put on your clothes and come along with me."

Instantly wide awake, Joe got off his cot and donned his clothes. Then he followed Al along the corridor, which was dimly lit by a small, yellowish bulb in the ceiling. Reaching the end of the hallway,

Ambrose unbolted the door and opened it. A blast of frigid arctic air rushed in.

Ambrose pointed out the door. "There are Frank and Commander Noonan," he said.

Joe advanced to the doorway and looked out. Suddenly something struck him on the head, and he was pushed out into the snow!

13 Rescued in Time

Joe hit the ground and lay there motionless for a second. Then he struggled to his feet. His head swimming, he pounded on the door, which had locked itself behind him.

"Open up! I can't get in!" he yelled as loud as he could. But the howling wind carried away the sound of his voice, and no one in the back of the building could hear his pounding.

The frigid cold bored through his light clothing and he shivered violently. He felt dizzy and blacked out momentarily, collapsing in the snow.

He came to when a hand slapped his face and a familiar voice shouted, "Joe! Come on, get up!"

The boy opened his eyes and saw his father standing over him!

"We're locked out," Joe muttered weakly.

"It doesn't matter," Fenton Hardy replied. "We'll spend the night in my Sno-Cat."

The Bayport sleuth helped his son across to the vehicle, pushed him in, and followed him into the cabin. The warmth soon brought Joe around. He stared in surprise when he saw his brother huddled in a corner with a blanket around him.

"Frank! How'd you get here?"

"Same as you," Frank responded. "I bet Ambrose told you Noonan wanted to see you, and then conked you on the head."

Joe nodded. "He figured he could get rid of both of us this way. In the morning, everyone would have thought we went outside and locked ourselves out by mistake."

"But Dad, what about you?" Frank inquired.

"I arrived just at the right time," Mr. Hardy replied. "I saw Frank being kicked out the door, so I brought him in here. Then Al pulled the same trick on you."

"What made you come to Outpost I?" Joe asked, while covering himself with a blanket his father handed him.

"Since I couldn't raise you on the radio, I decided to see whether you had arrived safely."

"We almost didn't," Frank said and reported what happened. "I think Muller sent us the wrong way deliberately!" he added.

"That only confirms my suspicion of him," Mr. Hardy said. "Here's what I found out. Muller wrote Admiral Langton a memo shortly after he arrived. Langton read it and put it in his desk. When he took it out the next morning, the writing had disappeared! He thought he must have made a mistake and put a blank sheet of paper in his desk. Since it was unimportant, he didn't pursue the matter."

"Muller wrote the note in disappearing ink," Frank concluded.

"Yes. The story interested me because a navy lab where Muller worked previously used pens containing disappearing ink for security reasons. But no one's authorized to take those pens anywhere else. Apparently Muller brought a few when he came here. I felt he might have wanted them to write messages for the theft ring."

"But why would he use such a pen on Langton's memo?" Joe inquired.

"He made a mistake," his father said. "I also found out he was stationed in San Diego for a while, and I suspect this was the headquarters of the gang for a long time."

"Al Ambrose is from San Diego!" Frank cried out.

Mr. Hardy nodded. "When the two got leery about being caught, they volunteered for service in the Antarctic. Now Muller is running the operation from here. I wasn't convinced that my theory was correct until I came here."

"You're right on target, Dad. When we left Byrd Base, Muller marked the location of Outpost I on our map. Later, the mark disappeared. We know the mark was in the wrong place to mislead us."

"We must have Muller arrested at once!" Joe urged.

"I've been working on that," his father said. "Unfortunately, the man left on an army transport plane for Punta Arenas this morning. Admiral Langton tells me it's all on the level, and that Muller was to go to San Diego on official business. But I suspect he'll use the opportunity to escape. Once we arrived on the scene, he must have sensed he was in great danger of being discovered. That's why he tried to get you two out of the way as fast as he could. I doubt he'll ever arrive in San Diego, but if he does, he'll be arrested."

"He must have radioed Al Ambrose before he left," Frank surmised. "Then, when we got here, Al realized that Muller's scheme to get rid of us had failed. So he tried on his own."

Mr. Hardy nodded. "We'll confront Ambrose

with the evidence in the morning. Right now I suggest we all get some sleep."

The trio huddled together, putting on every bit of clothing they could find to keep from freezing. Mr. Hardy turned the engine on every so often to warm up the cabin, but the rest of the night was far from comfortable for the Bayport sleuths.

In the morning, one of the men spotted the Sno-Cat through the window, and opened the door for them. After taking off their heavy clothing, they went into the dining room, where the crew of Outpost I was just arriving for breakfast.

Al Ambrose came in with a steaming pot of coffee. When he saw the Hardy boys, he stared at them as if they were ghosts, and the pot almost fell out of his hand.

"Morning, Al," Joe greeted him. "I can sure go for some ham and eggs."

"Especially after you kicked us out the door last night and we almost froze to death," Frank added. "If our father hadn't arrived in time, both Joe and I wouldn't be alive this morning!"

Ambrose gulped and began to tremble. Commander Noonan stared at him in surprise, then turned to the Hardys. "What on earth are you boys talking about?"

"I suggest that you put this man under arrest for

attempted murder of my sons, to which I was a witness," Mr. Hardy spoke up. "Then I'll tell you why I'm here."

Al dropped the coffee pot on the table and tried to run out of the room.

"Stop!" Noonan commanded. "Where do you think you're going? Out into the cold?"

Al realized that there was no way to escape. He meekly submitted to being handcuffed and was led out of the dining room.

The commander and Mr. Hardy disappeared into Noonan's private quarters and the detective reported what had happened. Noonan was dumbfounded and regretted deeply that one of his men was involved in the theft ring. An hour later, the three Hardys were on their way back to Byrd Base.

The Bayport detective drove his Sno-Cat with Ambrose locked in the rear. Frank and Joe followed in the vehicle they had brought to Outpost I.

Joe, who was at the wheel, commented, "It sure is easier going back than it was coming out. Of course, we know where we're going this time, and we have a better driver. Me."

"Don't run through a red light!" Frank quipped. "You might lose your Sno-Cat license."

When the group reached Byrd Base, Ambrose was taken into Admiral Langton's headquarters.

The young man confessed to being in league with Muller. He did not know, however, where Muller had gone.

"We tracked down the plane he was to take out of Punta Arenas," Langton said. "Apparently he never made the connection and disappeared."

"Well, it seems I have my next assignment cut out for me," Mr. Hardy said with a smile.

Langton nodded. "We're counting on you to find the man," he confirmed.

"Can we help?" Frank asked.

Mr. Hardy shook his head. "I can handle it on my own. Why don't you two go back to Santiago and see what you can find out about Julio Santana."

"We'll be glad to supply your transportation," Admiral Langton offered. "You've been a great help to us, and I regret that your lives were in such danger while you were here."

Frank grinned. "That's happened before," he said. "It's part of the job."

Early the next morning, the Hardy boys arrived in Punta Arenas. Before going any further, they decided to get in touch with Bertrand. The antique dealer told them that Santana had not been found yet.

"The police have had no luck so far," Bertrand said. "We're up against a blank wall. If you want to try again, why don't you come here and see what you can do?"

"We will," Frank promised. "But first we'd like to do a little sleuthing in Punta Arenas. Santana might be back here on his job as an oil driller."

After finishing the conversation with Bertrand, Frank called the local authorities and the company Santana had worked for. Nobody had seen or heard from the Easter Islander.

"What'll we do now?" Joe asked.

"We might as well go back to Santiago," Frank advised.

While waiting for a connecting flight, the boys walked through the lobby. Suddenly, Frank grabbed Joe by the elbow and pointed to a row of seats at the end of the room facing the wall. Two dark men were sitting on the aisle with passengers near them. They had their heads together and were holding an intense conversation.

"That's Santana!" Frank hissed. "And the other one's the guy who helped him overturn the bridge when we nearly fell into the gorge!"

14 Airport Chase

"What do you think he's doing in Punta Arenas?" Joe whispered.

Frank shrugged. "Let's follow him. Maybe we'll find out."

Adopting a casual air, the Hardys strolled across the waiting room, bought newspapers, and sat down behind Santana and his companion. They raised their papers as if reading, and strained their ears to hear what was being said.

However, the men were speaking Spanish in such low tones that the only thing they could make out was *Isla de Pascua*, which Frank knew meant Easter Island.

Suddenly Santana rose to his feet and walked past

the Hardys without noticing them. They got up and followed him through the waiting room, screening themselves by mingling with the crowd and staying just close enough to watch him.

Santana walked to the elevator, where he punched the button for the mezzanine. Realizing he was going up one flight, the boys immediately ran up the stairs. They positioned themselves against a low wall overlooking the waiting room, again shielded by their newspapers, and waited to see what would happen.

The elevator door opened and Santana emerged, walking over to a row of lockers. He took a key from his pocket, opened one, and removed a leather case. Then he walked away.

"Maybe he has the idol in there!" Joe hissed.

The boys hurried after the man, who seemed to sense their presence and looked back over his shoulder. When he recognized them, he rushed to the opposite side of the wall overlooking the waiting room. Frank and Joe followed, but at that moment, passengers flooded into the mezzanine from a plane that had just landed. The crowd crossed between the boys and Santana, who raced to the wall, called out something in Spanish, and tossed the case to his companion below in the waiting room.

The man caught it, clasped it tightly under his arm, and ran out an exit, while Santana headed for the stairs on the opposite side of the mezzanine.

Still held up by the crowd, Frank and Joe followed as fast as they could.

When they reached the stairs, they could see the fugitive going through a revolving door leading to the runways outside. Vaulting down the stairway, they dashed to the door, only to be stopped by two small children who got there first. They wedged themselves in with their mother behind them and moved the door slowly.

At last, the boys found themselves outside the terminal. Many planes were being serviced and a few were taxiing into position for takeoff. One was coming in for a landing.

A small craft stood on the nearest strip. On its side were stenciled the words *Inca Chief*. The Hardys could see the pilot preparing to leave.

"He's Santana's pal!" Joe gasped.

A passenger, whose face they could not distinguish, sat behind the man. Santana, running at top speed, reached the plane while the pilot revved the motor. He jumped in and slammed the door shut, then tapped his friend on the shoulder, pointing through the window at Frank and Joe. Obviously, he was telling his friend to hurry. At once, the plane began to move. A rush of exhaust fumes and dust deluged the boys as they raced up. Then the craft gathered speed, became airborne, and zoomed off into the sky!

The boys stopped in disgust and watched it vanish into the clouds.

"We've lost him again," said Joe. "He's as slippery as an eel in Barmet Bay."

"Let's see if we can find out where he's going," Frank suggested. "The pilot had to file a flight plan with air traffic control."

They went into the control tower, where the man in charge spoke several languages, including English. Frank explained that the Santiago police were looking for the man in the *Inca Chief,* and asked for the plane's destination.

The official consulted the records. "According to the flight plan filed by Pedro Morena, the pilot, the *Inca Chief* is headed for Easter Island," he told them.

Thanking him, the Hardys went back to the terminal, and Frank phoned the police. The lieutenant they had spoken to earlier listened to his report on Santana.

"I will radio Easter Island at once," he promised. "Santana will be arrested as soon as his plane lands."

"Now what'll we do?" Joe asked after his brother had hung up.

"We'll try to get a flight to Easter Island," Frank said. "But first, let's tell Bertrand what happened."

The antique dealer was disappointed that Santana had escaped again, but agreed with the boys that they should follow him.

"I know Easter Island," he said, "so I can tell you what to do. Fly into Hanga Roa, the capital. Stay at the Hanga Roa Hotel, and go to the governor's residence and tell him why you're there. He'll help you with everything."

"Santana and his buddy should be in the lockup when we get there," Frank observed.

"I hope so!" Bertrand said fervently. "You boys have to retrieve our idol!"

Since there were no commercial flights to Easter Island, Frank and Joe found a charter pilot who was willing to take them. Before boarding, Joe bought a guidebook on Easter Island, while Frank selected a copy of Thor Heyerdahl's *Aku-Aku*.

"Easter Island's more than two thousand miles off the coast of Chile," Joe said. "From down here, it'll be even farther. We're in for a long flight."

After the pilot had taken off, the boys studied the guidebook. They discovered that Easter Island was quite small, only fifteen miles by eleven, with a population of about two thousand people. "It has a number of extinct volcanos," Joe announced, "the most important being Mount Rano Raraku where the natives got the volcanic stone from which they carved their giant figures."

Frank smiled. "That's one thing I've been wanting to see for a long time, and thought I never would. The stone heads of Easter Island!"

"I know one thing you won't see," Joe said. "Trees!"

"You mean there are none on the island?"

"That's right. Only grass. Sheepherding is one of the leading industries, but many natives make a living from the growing tourist trade."

"Well," Frank quipped, "in that case, the only place Santana can hide is in a volcano!"

15 The Wizard

As they were thundering along over the ocean, Frank flipped through the pages of *Aku-Aku*.

"This book is great," he said. "Tells about Thor Heyerdahl's expedition. He wanted to solve the mysteries of the island, which he did. Some of them, anyhow. Like that business of the long ears on the statues. He says the Incas who came from South America had long ears. So when they made the carvings, they gave them long ears."

"But why did they produce those big stone figures?" Joe asked.

"That's one mystery Heyerdahl didn't solve. He says no one knows why they created them or how they transported them from Mount Rano Raraku. Some weigh fifty tons! Look at this picture."

Frank pointed to an illustration of Heyerdahl sitting on top of a stone figure twenty feet tall. Other illustrations showed giant carvings lying on the ground near platforms on which they had once stood.

"Who knocked them over?" Joe wondered.

"Invaders from across the Pacific, Heyerdahl thinks," Frank replied. "They came from Polynesia and conquered Easter Island. To demonstrate they were the bosses, they pushed the statues off the platforms. That's the way it was when a Dutch sea captain discovered the island in the eighteenth century. Later, Captain Cook landed there during his voyage around the world. Finally, Chile annexed the place in the nineteenth century."

Their conversation was interrupted by their pilot, who offered them sandwiches that he had brought along.

"Oh, I'm so glad you thought of that," Joe said. "I'm starved!"

After their meal, they slept for several hours until at last Easter Island came in sight. The plane circled over the area, and the Hardys got a broad view of rolling, grass-covered terrain. They looked down into the craters of extinct volcanos and noticed that high cliffs fell off into the water along most of the coast.

Over the airfield, Joe commented, "No planes on

the ground. The *Inca Chief* must have left already. I hope they arrested Santana when he arrived!"

After landing, the Hardys went to the control tower and asked about Santana's plane.

"According to the flight plan of pilot Pedro Morena, that plane's overdue," said a man at the monitoring control board. "I'll see if I can raise him on the radio."

He lifted the transmitter and called, "Easter Island control to *Inca Chief!* Come in, please! Pedro Morena, come in, please!" He repeated the call several times, then set the transmitter aside.

"No answer," he reported.

"Will you let us know what happens?" Frank asked. "We'll be at the Hanga Roa Hotel."

"As soon as we know," the man promised.

"Thanks. Our names are Frank and Joe Hardy."

The boys retraced their steps just in time to catch the bus to the hotel at the southeastern end of Easter Island. They found the capital was a town of tiny houses, where most of the people on Easter Island lived. The hotel was small but modern. After being shown to their room, they debated their next move.

"There isn't much we can do tonight," Frank said. "But we should report to the governor right away. He's the one who can make sure Santana's taken into custody when the *Inca Chief* lands. Anyway, we'll have to let him know what we're doing here."

"You're right," Joe agreed. "Let's go find him. Shouldn't be too hard. Hanga Roa is a small place."

After getting directions at the hotel desk, the brothers walked to a bungalow south of Hanga Roa where the governor of Easter Island resided. Chile's flag flew from a flagpole, but there was no activity at the building.

"I guess we're the only ones who have business with the governor tonight," Joe said. "Things are rather informal around here."

A servant showed them into the official's office. The governor was a middle-aged man wearing the uniform of a captain in Chile's army. He shook hands with Frank and Joe, gestured them to be seated, and settled down behind his desk.

"What can I do for you?" he inquired in fluent English.

The boys explained that they were looking for Santana and the stone idol. Frank showed him the photograph of the sculpture that Kimberley had given them.

"I know about this," the governor responded. "The police called me. I will interrogate Santana as soon as the *Inca Chief* arrives. The control tower at the airfield informs me that the plane is overdue. Of course, the pilot may have changed his plans or had trouble and set down somewhere else."

"Governor, do you know anything about the stone idol?" Frank inquired.

"I never signed a receipt for its removal from the island," the man replied. "In fact, I never saw it."

"We were told a Scandinavian collector bought it," Joe pointed out.

The governor shook his head. "I know nothing about this man or how he got the idol. I suggest you see a man named Iko Hiva, who's the leader of the people of Easter Island. He's considered a wizard, and if anyone knows anything about the idol, Iko Hiva does."

"We'd like to talk to him," Frank said.

The governor gave them directions to the man's home, and the following morning after breakfast, Frank and Joe walked to the outskirts of Hanga Roa. They stopped at a hut with a grinning skull over the front door.

"I wonder who that is," Frank muttered. "Or was!"

"No point asking him," Joe quipped. "He's not about to invite us in."

The boy knocked and heard a shuffling of feet approaching inside of the hut. Then the door swung open. The face of a hideous monster confronted them! Its eyes glared savagely, and its mouth was twisted in an evil leer!

Startled by the apparition, the boys stood rooted to the spot. Suddenly, the figure's right hand reached up and pulled the face off. An old man grinned at them. "Welcome!" he said.

Frank was flustered. "Eh, do you always greet your visitors in disguise, with that awful mask on?"

"It is the image of one of the ancient gods of Easter Island," the man said in English. He was slightly built with wrinkled brown skin and coal black eyes. He wore a checkered shirt, canvas trousers, and sneakers.

"I am Iko Hiva," the man went on without answering the question. "I can see you are Americans. I learned your language at school. Why have you come to see me?"

The Hardys introduced themselves.

"We want to talk to you about a stone idol," Joe explained.

Iko Hiva shrugged. "I know more about the idols of Easter Island than anyone else. Come in."

The boys entered the hut. They found themselves in a single large room with neither table nor chairs. Stone figures with misshapen features were displayed on shelves along the walls, and a number of hideous masks hung from strings attached to the ceiling.

A block of black, volcanic stone rose three feet from the floor under one window. On it lay a long stone knife. A primitive fishing spear leaned at an angle against the block.

There was a musty smell in the room because, despite Easter Island's warm temperature, all the windows were closed and locked.

Frank thought to himself, the governor said this guy was a wizard. Weirdo's more like it!

Aloud he said, "A man named Julio Santana has the idol we're looking for. Do you know him?"

Iko Hiva stroked his chin. "I know him. He used to be an important man on the island, a defender of our gods and our traditions. He left to find work elsewhere. But I have communicated with him recently."

The Hardys stared at him. "You've corresponded with him?" Frank asked.

Iko Hiva shook his head. "I spoke to him in spirit."

The boys felt disappointed, but said nothing.

"Do you know the Scandinavian collector who brought the idol from Easter Island?" Joe asked.

"I do not. But so many collectors come to our island that it is possible I failed to notice him. He did not come to me. What is your interest in him?"

"He sold the idol to South American Antiquities, who commissioned us to find it after Santana stole it," Frank said.

Iko Hiva looked thoughtful. "We have many

stone idols. Describe the one you are looking for, and perhaps I can help you."

"We can do better than that," Frank replied and took the photograph from his pocket, handing it to Iko Hiva. The wizard frowned as he gazed at the face with the circular eyes, broad nose, and long ears.

"This is the guardian of the sacred cave!" he cried.

"Is that important?" Joe queried.

"Of course it is! The guardian was on the altar of the sacred cave for centuries. It disappeared but a short while ago!"

"Maybe an Easter Islander sold it to the Scandinavian collector," Frank suggested.

"Never! No one would touch it!"

"Why not?"

"The *aku-aku* would take revenge on him!"

16 Guardian of the Sacred Cave

A strange feeling came over the Hardys as Iko Hiva spoke. A tingling sensation ran up and down Frank's spine, and the hair rose on the back of Joe's neck.

"The *aku-aku* protects the guardian of the sacred cave," the man shouted. "None of our people would have taken the idol. It must have been stolen from the altar by an outsider. No one has any right to it. Do you intend to keep it from us?"

"No, we don't," Frank assured him hastily. "If what you say is true, we'll see the idol stays on Easter Island. But if the sculpture was legally sold by someone in authority, we have to return it to South American Antiquities."

"All we want right now," Joe put in, "is to find the

idol. Since you want to find it too, why can't we work together?"

Iko Hiva calmed down. "I will tell you what I will do. I will take you to the sacred cave and you can see for yourselves the altar where the idol used to stand."

The wizard led the boys out the back door to a corral where three horses were grazing. A number of saddles hung on the fence.

"Can you boys ride?" he asked.

"Sure. We ride a lot at home in Bayport," Joe replied.

"Well, then, saddle up and we will go."

When the mounts were ready, the old man set out at a quick canter, followed by Frank and Joe. The ride took them about two miles to the coast and then south along a steep cliff where they passed an extinct volcano with stone ruins near the summit.

"That is Mount Rano Kao," said Iko Hiva. "The ruins are those of Orongo, the place where our bird men used to celebrate their rites. Some of them still haunt Orongo," he added darkly.

The wizard pulled his horse to a stop on the edge of a steep cliff and pointed across the water to an island. "That is Motunui where the terns nest. The bird men used to race down from Orongo, across to Motunui, and greet the terns flying in. That was the source of their magical power. It still is."

The wizard dismounted a short while later and tied the reins of his horse to a stake driven into the ground. Frank and Joe did the same.

Then Iko Hiva led the way to a point where a rope ladder dangled down the cliff for about fifty feet. Frank judged it was a thousand feet from the end of the rope ladder to the pounding surf below. The ladder swung in the breeze, its rungs clattering against the cliff.

"Climb down until you see an opening in the wall," Iko Hiva instructed the boys. "That is the entrance of the sacred cave. Follow the tunnel in and you will find the altar. There is not sufficient room for three, so I will stay here."

Frank edged himself over the brink first. Getting a grip on the top rung with his hands, he found a lower rung with his feet and began the descent. Joe came after him. Rung by rung, they worked their way down the swaying ladder along the side of the cliff while the sound of the foaming surf echoed in their ears.

The mouth of the cave was directly to their left. Frank went in first with Joe right behind him. When they reached the tunnel, they had to get down on their hands and knees, and finally wriggled forward on their stomachs. Soon they were in total darkness.

"What's the point of this?" Joe muttered. "We

wouldn't be able to see the altar if we fell over it."

"Maybe the old man laid a trap for us," Frank said uneasily. "Wait—there's a light up ahead."

The way began to broaden until the boys were able to move on their hands and knees again. The light became stronger as they rounded a corner and saw a strange sight.

The passage ended in a circular opening too narrow for them to slip through. It was guarded by a circle of stone knives fastened into the rock. Beyond the knives there was a block of volcanic rock on which stood seven sputtering candles, three on each side and one in the center.

A shelf cut into the earth next to the Hardys held unused candles, wooden tongs for reaching them past the knives onto the altar, and long tapers for lighting the candles when they were in place.

Frank tried the edge of one of the knives with his thumb.

"Sharp as a razor," he declared. "Anyone reaching in there would sure give himself a shave."

"Well, *somebody* got the stone idol off the altar," Joe said, "and not with those tongs, either. They're not strong enough to hold it."

Agreeing there was nothing more they could learn in the sacred cave, the Hardys slowly backed down the tunnel until they reached the rope ladder.

Mounting it, they rejoined Iko Hiva at the top of the cliff.

"I replace the candles when they burn down too far," he told them. "The idol used to stand in the middle of the altar. I am desperate to get it back. Can you help me?"

"We'll try," Frank promised.

The wizard nodded. "I want you to see Rano Raraku. You will learn more about the traditions of Easter Island. It is ten miles away in the northeast."

The three climbed back in the saddle and rode around the base of Rano Kao before turning their horses onto a long trail up the coast. They passed natives and Chilean officials traveling on horseback, in jeeps, or on foot. Statues were lying on the ground beside stone platforms. Iko Hiva pointed out more caves where the ancient population used to hide from their enemies.

The Hardys recognized Rano Raraku when they spotted it from down the trail because many famous stone figures stood in the earth on the flanks of the extinct volcano.

The three reined in their horses and looked at the mysterious figures with their oval eyes, broad noses, pursed lips, and long ears.

"They are the sentinels of Rano Raraku," said Iko Hiva solemnly. "They have been here since the beginning of time. They are telling us that the ancient traditions of Easter Island must not be violated. I am in mystic communication with them," he added.

Maneuvering their horses between the uncanny stone giants, the three rode up the slope to the summit and peered over the edge into the crater that once hurled forth dense clouds of suffocating smoke and rivers of molten lava.

When the volcano had stopped erupting, the lava had cooled and become hard, black rock. The boys could see how the Easter Islanders cut the rock into blocks from which they carved their weird statues. Some half-finished sculptures still lay in the crater, reminders that work had ceased when the Polynesians conquered the island.

"How did those statues get all over the island?" Frank asked, remembering Thor Heyerdahl's account that they had been moved to different points.

"They got where they are by themselves," the wizard replied.

"But they have no legs!"

"They flew through the air. Some stayed near Rano Raraku. Others continued to the platforms built for them along the coast."

"Why were they thrown off the platforms?" Joe asked.

Iko Hiva scowled. "A witch did it. Her magic was too powerful for the statues. They fell and were unable to get up again. Fortunately, the sentinels of Rano Raraku were strong enough to repel the witch's spell. That is why they are still standing."

The Hardys surveyed the area, noting that there was a lake at the bottom of the crater. Several boys were either swimming in the water or paddling reed boats over the surface.

"All of the old fire mountains have crater lakes," Iko Hiva explained. "We get our water from them because there are no streams on Easter Island. Do you wish to see more?"

Frank shook his head, recalling that he and Joe should be getting back to the hotel to see if there was any word on the *Inca Chief.*

"I will help you as much as I can," Iko Hiva promised. "If you need a wizard's power, call on me!"

He turned his horse down the slopes of Rano Raraku and led the ride back to Hanga Roa. This time they passed flocks of sheep and saw shepherds guarding them.

At Iko Hiva's hut, the Hardys unsaddled their horses, thanked the old man, and walked to the Hanga Roa Hotel. Since there was no message at the desk, Frank phoned the airport.

"We still have not heard from the *Inca Chief*," he was told. "The pilot must have interrupted his flight. But not long ago a blip appeared on our radar, then vanished from the screen. If it was the *Inca Chief*, I fear it has crashed into the ocean!"

17 The Bird Man

"We are in the process of starting an air and sea search," the voice continued.

"Please keep us posted," Frank said, and with a troubled frown, hung up.

"If the *Inca Chief* went down," he said to Joe, "we'll never see Santana again."

"Or the stone idol, Frank. Anyway, we can't leave Easter Island until we know for sure."

The phone rang. "Maybe that's the control tower now!" Joe exclaimed as he lifted the instrument to his ear.

A muffled voice said, "Hardys, if you want to know about the stone idol, be at Orongo before dawn!"

Then there was a click and Joe put down the receiver.

"That was a quick one," Frank commented. "You didn't say a word."

"I didn't have a chance." Joe repeated what he had heard.

"Did you recognize the voice?" Frank asked.

Joe shook his head. "It sounded as if he was holding a handkerchief over the mouthpiece. He could be anybody who knows we're looking for the stone idol."

"Maybe he's an Easter Islander who can tell us about it but doesn't want anyone else to know," Frank conjectured. "Iko Hiva could have spread the word around that we're interested in the idol. Or a servant in the governor's residence might have overheard us mention the idol last night."

"It could also be someone who wants to get rid of us!" Joe pointed out.

"I know. But I still think we should go to Orongo."

The boys spent the afternoon strolling around Hanga Roa, then had dinner at the hotel. A message that the search for the *Inca Chief* had been fruitless was awaiting them.

"Perhaps they'll go out again tomorrow," Joe said.

Frank nodded morosely, then suggested that they

go to the governor and tell him of their plans to meet their unknown contact at Orongo.

"It could be a trap," the governor agreed. "I will send a policeman after you if you have not returned by early morning."

"That would be great," Frank said. "Thanks."

"Call me as soon as you get back from your mysterious rendezvous," the governor added, and the boys left.

They set their alarm for three o'clock, then went to sleep. Later, in the darkness, they walked to Rano Kao and climbed up to Orongo. By now a full moon flooded light over the ruins, casting weird shadows on the ground. A dark patch showed the entrance to a cave used by the bird men in olden times.

"The Easter Islanders sure were big on this kind of thing," Frank commented.

"Real cave men," Joe quipped.

They came to a jumble of massive rocks decorated with weird figures. Many were of men with the heads of birds, their bodies twisted out of shape, their heads uplifted to reveal their long curving beaks. There were cryptic hieroglyphic marks on some of the rocks.

"Our friend on the phone sure chose a spooky place to meet," Joe grumbled.

"Maybe he wants to be sure we're alone. Thor Heyerdahl found that most Easter Islanders would not come up here at night. They're afraid the spirits of Orongo would get them."

Joe looked at the sky. "I hope we don't have to wait too long. This place gives me the creeps."

"Not scared of the bird men, are you?" Frank joked.

"No, but there are lots of places I'd rather be."

The boys found a protected spot and sat down with their backs against an outcropping of rock. They discussed the strange phone call.

"I just can't make any sense of it," Frank said. "But we've got to wait here until—" He broke off suddenly as the moonlight threw a sinister shadow on the ground in front of them.

Jumping to their feet, they whirled around and saw a man with the head of a bird perched on the rock overhead!

Holding a black volcanic rock in each hand, the uncanny apparition leaped on the Hardys, struck each on the head, and knocked them to the ground! Then their attacker ran off into the darkness.

Frank and Joe lay stunned where they had fallen, but gradually recovered. Sitting up, they rubbed their heads, wincing as their fingers touched the bumps where the stones had struck.

"We were ambushed!" Joe groaned. "It must have been the guy on the phone!"

"He's trying to scare us away from Easter Island, I bet," Frank added. "No doubt he's afraid we'll find the truth about the stone idol!"

"That means we're getting warm. But I still don't see how."

"Neither do I. By the way, what happened to our bird man? He sure flew away in a hurry."

"Maybe not," Joe said in an undertone. He pointed to the mouth of the Orongo cave. "He could be hiding in there. Let's go see!"

Grabbing a rock to use as a weapon, he slipped into the cave and began to work his way on hands and knees through a narrow tunnel, using his flashlight to see ahead of him. Frank followed close behind.

"This place gives me claustrophobia!" Joe muttered. "Anyway, the bird man can't ambush us in here. There's no place for him to hide."

The tunnel was short and they came to the end in a couple of minutes.

"No one here," Joe called over his shoulder. "Reverse gears."

Frank backed up as rapidly as he could. Joe was slower. Suddenly a shower of rocks fell between the boys! Frank was safe near the mouth of the cave, but his brother was trapped underground!

Frantically Frank threw himself on the barrier. As fast as he could, he dug into it, throwing rocks over his shoulder. When he removed a big boulder near the top of the pile, he created an aperture through to the other side.

"Joe! Can you hear me?" Frank shouted.

"Loud and clear!"

"Hold on, I'll get you out." The young detective removed the rest of the debris, taking care not to start another rock slide. Finally Joe was able to wriggle through and they both emerged from the cave.

"Do you think the bird man did that?" Joe said after he breathed in a lungful of fresh air.

"I doubt it," Frank said. "I was already near the entrance and didn't hear or see anyone. I think the rocks just caved in. Maybe no one has used the cave in a long time, and the movement we made inside caused some of the ceiling to shift."

"Well, that's the last cave I'll ever go into!" Joe vowed. "The chances we take to find Santana!"

Just then, a voice sounded behind them. Whirling around, they went into a defensive stance and prepared to meet another attack by the bird man. Instead, a friendly Easter Islander was walking toward them. On his shirt, he wore an official-looking badge.

"He must be the policeman the governor promised to send after us," Joe said.

The man said something in his native dialect, ending with, "Santana?"

"Do you know about Santana?" Joe asked eagerly.

The man nodded. He pointed to the shore, gestured to the Hardys to go with him, and walked off.

"Maybe the *Inca Chief* arrived, or they found the wreck offshore," Frank surmised. "Let's see where he's taking us."

They followed the Easter Islander from Orongo to the cliff below. A narrow trail enabled them to reach the bottom where surf pounded over massive rocks. An outrigger canoe, with a spear and hand net inside, was drawn up to the shore.

"He's a fisherman," Joe said. "They probably don't even have full-time cops around here."

The man pointed to the island of Motunui across the water.

"Is Santana there?" Frank asked.

The man nodded. Pushing the canoe off the rocks into the surf, he climbed aboard and gestured to the Hardys to join him.

When they got in, he handed them a couple of paddles and took one himself. He sat up front and gave the boys a lead as the three dug their paddles into the water and started the canoe toward Motunui.

The small craft pitched up and down in the waves, maintaining its balance by means of the outrigger on one side, which stablized it and prevented it from turning over. The Hardys had experience with most types of boats, and had no trouble keeping up with the fisherman. The going got easier as they reached the placid water beyond the surf.

They crossed about a mile of open ocean before arriving at Motunui. Frank and Joe were preparing to jump out and help drag the canoe onto the beach, but the Easter Islander shook his head and pointed to a smaller island on the right. They turned in that direction, entered the surf of the little patch of land, and beached the canoe.

Curious, the Hardys followed their guide inland.

"Joe, be ready for anything," Frank warned. "Santana plays rough. He sure did with us in the Andes."

"I know. But I hope he's already in the hands of the police."

The man led them to a stone chapel, which had broken windows and grass growing around its foundation. The door hung crazily on one hinge.

"This place hasn't been used for years," Frank muttered.

"Where's Santana?" he asked their guide apprehensively.

The native pointed to an inscription on the stone above the doorway. The Hardys looked at it and read the words *Santa Ana*.

"Oh, no!" Joe groaned.

Frank grinned in spite of his disappointment. "He must have heard us talking about Santana when he walked up to us and figured this is what we wanted to see. Santa Ana and Santana do sound alike."

Suddenly a noise that seemed like a footstep came from within the building.

"Someone's in there!" Joe cried.

He and Frank rushed toward the door. As they reached it, a man with the head of a bird plunged between the boys, ran around the corner, and vanished!

18 *The* Inca Chief

The Hardys ran after the bird man. Rounding the abandoned chapel, they saw him dashing for the beach, where a reed boat was drawn up. Quickly they closed the gap and had almost overtaken him when he suddenly turned and tripped Joe.

The boy fell heavily to the ground, but Frank reached out and put a headlock on the fugitive. They struggled violently for a moment, then the man wrenched loose from his disguise. Frank was left holding the bird headdress and the man shoved him into the sand. Then the man jumped into the reed boat and paddled away furiously.

Frank got to his feet as Joe ran up to him. "Outwitted again," he muttered angrily. "There he goes, and all we have are his stupid feathers!"

"Did you recognize him?" Joe asked.

Frank nodded. "He's Pedro Morena, Santana's pilot!"

"That means the *Inca Chief* didn't crash after all!" Joe cried out. "Let's see if we can catch up with Morena in the canoe!"

The boys ran back to their guide, who still stood near the chapel, an expression of fear on his face.

Frank used a sort of sign language to explain that they wanted to pursue the fugitive, but the man shook his head. He pointed to the headdress in Frank's hand and waved his hand to indicate his refusal.

"He's afraid of the bird man," Frank interpreted. He was proven right when the Easter Islander would not let them into the boat with the bird man's feathers. Finally Frank put the headdress on the chapel steps and their guide reluctantly indicated he would take them back to Easter Island.

When they passed Motunui, Joe spotted something gleaming in the sunlight beyond the crest of a small hill. "Hey, Frank," he said and pointed. "I wonder what that is."

Frank shielded his eyes with his hand. "Let's check it out."

They signaled their guide to paddle ashore, then strode to the top of the hill and looked down on the other side. A small plane was parked at the end of a level plain below, and on its side were the words *Inca Chief!*

"So this is where Morena and Santana landed," Frank cried out. "They maintained radio silence and came down secretly on this deserted island. Easy enough for a small plane."

"It zipped right past the radar," Joe added. "They fooled the guy in the control tower when the blip went off the screen. We'll have to get back to Hanga Roa and tell the authorities."

"First let's give the *Inca Chief* the once over and drain the fuel tank in case Morena comes back to fly out after we leave."

The Hardys advanced cautiously toward the plane. When they got close enough, they saw through a window that it was empty. Pulling the door open, they got in and searched the interior.

Joe opened a leather case he found on the floor. "This is what Santana took out of the locker in Punta Arenas," he declared. "If the idol was ever in here, it sure isn't now. As a matter of fact, it isn't anywhere in the plane," he added after an exhaustive search of the cabin.

Finding the key still in the lock, Frank turned on the motor, which erupted into action for a moment and then died.

"Now I know why Morena left the key," the boy commented. "The fuel tank's empty. He must have just made it here. A few minutes more and both of them would have landed in the ocean."

Joe nodded. "But one thing puzzles me."

"What's that?"

"What was Morena doing on the island next door with that goofy birdman outfit?"

"I think I have the answer to that," Frank replied. "He was on the island for some reason of his own, and saw us approaching. Apparently he had his disguise with him, so he quickly put it on and tried his scaring act to frighten us away from the area and protect the hiding place of his plane."

The Hardys got out and scouted around the island, which was less than half a mile across in each direction. The lack of trees gave them a clear view, and they quickly realized that they and their guide were the only people on it.

"Let's make tracks for Hanga Roa," Frank suggested. "We don't have to leave a guard on the *Inca Chief*. It's not going anywhere."

They climbed back into the outrigger canoe and crossed over to Easter Island. After paying the fisherman with a handful of Chilean coins, they went directly to the governor's residence, where they were shown into his study.

"I am glad to see you safe and sound," he said with a smile. "Did my man find you?"

"He did," Joe replied. "He also helped us indirectly to find the *Inca Chief!*"

"What!" the governor was dumbfounded. "Our search was futile and we finally gave up looking for the plane!"

"The pilot landed on Motunui," Frank explained. "We almost caught him, but he escaped."

"What about Julio Santana?" the governor asked.

"He must be around here somewhere," Frank said. "But we have no idea where."

"There was also another passenger on board when they left Punta Arenas," Joe put in. "I don't know whether he was dropped off along the coast or whether he came here."

"Well, your investigation has been a success so far," the governor declared. "I will have the *Inca Chief* brought to the airfield and held there. And I will order a search for Morena and Santana and their passenger. I talked to the leading citizens of Easter Island. They are sure none of the natives stole the idol. That Scandinavian collector must have taken it himself!"

The Hardys promised to help the police in looking for the suspect, and then returned to the Hanga Roa Hotel.

"How about some chow?" Joe suggested. "We haven't had anything all day."

"Good thinking. Let's see what the chef can rustle up for us."

When they went and asked the man in charge of the kitchen, he smiled. "I see you are Americans," he said. "Perhaps you would like hamburgers? Most Americans do."

"Great!" Frank said. "And soda, if you have it."

"We have that, too. Every week we get supplies from Santiago."

Minutes later, Frank and Joe were on their way to their rooms. They sat down on their beds, placed their hamburgers and soda on the night table in between, and plunged into their meal with gusto.

After a while, Frank said, "What do you suppose Santana's up to? He's got the stone idol, but what's he doing with it? And why did he sneak into Easter Island like this?"

"He may have sold the stone idol," Joe pointed out. "We don't know for sure that he brought it here. On the other hand, he might be in cahoots with Iko Hiva. The wizard wants the idol back, and as long as Santana is willing to give it to him, Iko Hiva in turn might help our friend to get away from us."

Frank took a sip from his glass. "Santana can't hide for long on Easter Island. It's too small. And he can't get away either without his plane. By now, he must know we spotted Morena."

Joe munched his last bite of hamburger. "What about that passenger they had on the plane?" he asked. "Could he have anything to do with the stone sculpture?"

Frank shrugged. "I have no idea. I couldn't see his features at all. Perhaps he's another relative of Santana's."

"What'll we do next?"

"Let's walk around town and see if we can pick up a clue as to where Santana and Morena are hiding out," Frank suggested.

The young detectives scoured the area all afternoon, but found it difficult to communicate with the natives. And there was no sign of the two men anywhere.

In the morning, as they were coming out of the dining room after breakfast, they saw Iko Hiva sitting in the lobby.

"I have been waiting for you," the wizard declared. "I have something important to tell you."

"What is it?" Frank asked.

"The stone idol is back!"

19 Explanations

"What!" The Hardys were thunderstruck.

"The guardian once more stands on the altar in the sacred cave!" Iko Hiva went on. "I went in this morning to replace the candles and there it was. I hope you will come with me and see for yourselves."

"Of course," Joe agreed. "We've chased that sculpture a long way, and we don't want to leave without seeing it where it belongs."

"Good. A friend of mine has brought a car. He will drive us." Iko Hiva led the way outside, where he introduced the boys to another Easter Islander, who was at the wheel of a jeep. The newcomer did not speak English, but, with a friendly smile, he waved for the Hardys to climb into the back of the jeep.

When they arrived at the cliff, a crowd was gathered near the rope ladder. Two men were climbing up.

"The idol sure is popular," Joe commented.

Iko Hiva nodded. "The people are relieved to know it is back. They came down here as soon as I announced its return. Well, nobody is using the rope ladder now. I suggest you go into the sacred cave."

"Joe, what about your vow to stay away from caves?" Frank teased.

Joe grinned. "I've got the *aku-aku* on my side this time. That's good enough for me. I'll even show you the way, Frank."

Descending the ladder, the boys reached the entrance to the sacred cave. They crawled through the tunnel in the darkness until they saw the light at the opposite end. At last, they reached the opening guarded by the circle of stone knives.

Seven new candles were burning brightly on the altar, and the stone figure stood in front of the center candle!

A feeling of awe came over Frank and Joe as they gazed at the features they had seen before in the photograph. The circular eyes glinted at them in the flickering light, and the fierce scowl seemed to threaten them. The long ears reached to a level with the chin and looked more sinister now than in the office of South American Antiquities back in Santiago.

"You know something," Frank said, staring at the idol. "I don't think he likes us."

"I don't think he likes anybody," Frank muttered. "Let's get out of here before he puts the whammy on us."

They went back through the tunnel to the mouth of the cave and mounted the ladder to the top of the cliff. The crowd was growing bigger as more people arrived to view the stone idol. Frank and Joe climbed back into the jeep, and their driver started the return trip to Hanga Roa.

"So you see, the guardian of the sacred cave has come back to us," Iko Hiva declared.

"Who put it on the altar?" Joe inquired.

"The *aku-aku*," the wizard replied solemnly.

An *aku-aku* named Julio Santana, Frank thought.

"You will not try to take it away?" the old man went on.

"No," Joe assured him. "Not unless we can prove it was sold legitimately. But in order to do that, we'll have to find the Scandinavian collector who sold it to South American Antiquities. He didn't want his identity revealed, but at this point he has no choice."

The wizard smiled. "That is good. Now you do not have to fear the *aku-aku*."

Frank spoke up. "What if someone steals the idol again? The *aku-aku* couldn't prevent it before and might not be able to do it now."

Iko Hiva smiled. "Someone will always guard the cave in the future," he declared.

When they arrived at the hotel, the boys said good-bye to the wizard and his companion, then went inside. In their room, they discussed the latest developments.

"Santana must have put the idol back last night," Frank noted. "He was probably in the sacred cave while we were having our go-round with Morena at Orongo. The bird man stuff was a setup to get us out of the way. I bet it was either Santana or Morena on the phone who disguised his voice and tricked us into going to Orongo."

"Then perhaps Santana's not a thief, Frank! We thought he stole the idol after we found it because he wanted to sell it. Maybe he only wanted to bring it back where it belonged!"

"You're right," Frank said. "Someone else could have stolen it from Kimberley's bag in the hotel room, and hidden it in the secret compartment."

"And who took it from the sacred cave in the first place?"

Frank sighed. "For a minute, I thought we'd solved the puzzle, but now we have more questions than ever."

"Bertrand's still a suspect," Joe declared firmly. "He had the opportunity to take the idol in the hotel room. And he had a motive if he was trying to incriminate Kimberley and grab control of the business."

A knock on the door interrupted the discussion. Joe opened it up and gasped.

Julio Santana stood on the threshold!

"May I come in?" he asked pleasantly.

"Sure," Joe offered. "We were just talking about you."

"I can understand that," Santana admitted as he sat down. "Much has happened since we met in Santiago."

"Like you and Morena trying to knock us off the bridge into the gorge," Frank suggested.

"And fixing our brakes so we'd crack up in the Andes," Joe added. "Then you disguised your voice on the phone last night and sent your bird man to ambush us at Orongo."

"You're right," Santana admitted. "But I can explain everything. First of all, I did not tell Morena to attack you. I merely wanted him to frighten you away from Easter Island."

"Why?" Frank demanded.

"I thought you were here to steal the stone idol again. But Iko Hiva just told me you agree it must remain in the sacred cave. So I have come to apologize for mistrusting you. But you must understand that I felt *you* had stolen the idol when I saw you with it at South American Antiquities. I assumed you and Bertrand were going to sell it illegally. So I seized it and ran. I had to do everything in my power to protect it."

"Even if it meant killing us?" Joe challenged.

"When we followed you into the Andes, you decided to finish us off," Frank added.

"Remember, I thought you were thieves. Anyone who takes a sacred idol is not worthy of living. But the *aku-aku* knew better and protected you. So, you were never in real danger!"

"Why were you selling sculptures at the stand in your village square?" Frank inquired.

"I had watched you all the time," Santana revealed. "I saw you disguise yourselves at Ata Copac's house and set out for my village. I knew a shortcut and rushed home before you arrived. Then I asked Pedro to let me take over the stall."

"But what made you think we'd stop there?"

Santana smiled. "Anyone looking for a stone figurine would be interested in similar items. I intended to trap you by making you appear as thieves. The villagers have stern punishment for

people like that. But you escaped and I went back to
Santiago until Pedro could fly me here. He used to
be in the Chilean air force and has his pilot's
license."

"Why couldn't he take you right then?" Frank
asked.

"He was in the process of buying the *Inca Chief*,
which he will use for charters. I had to wait until
the transfer was completed."

"What were you doing in Punta Arenas?" Joe
inquired.

"Pedro had a fare to drop off first. Then we
stopped along the coast before we came to Easter
Island."

"How did you know the stone idol had been
taken from the sacred cave?"

"Iko Hiva wrote and told me while I was working
in the oil fields at Punta Arenas."

So Iko Hiva didn't communicate only in spirit as
he said, Joe thought. He's a wizard who pushes a
pen. I guess he didn't want us to know about it until
he figured out what we were up to.

"You see," Santana went on, "I grew up here,
knowing the stone idol as the guardian of the sacred
cave. Only the sacrilegious would touch it. When I
heard it was gone, I resolved to get it back at any
cost. Since South American Antiquities handles

more Easter Island artifacts than anybody else, I went to their office and applied for a job."

"And, fortunately, Bertrand needed a chauffeur," Joe said.

Santana nodded. "I took care of the company cars while trying to find the idol. You got it before I did. That is when I went into action."

"You didn't know it was in the possession of South American Antiquities before that moment?"

"No. I still don't know how they obtained it."

"Supposedly it was sold to Mr. Kimberley by a Scandinavian collector," Joe said.

Santana shrugged. "It's possible. But what I don't understand is why you pursued me. I thought you were doing research on the ancient Incas."

"That was our cover story," Frank told him. "We're really detectives. Mr. Kimberley hired us to find the idol, which had disappeared from his handbag."

"Now I understand," Santana said. "When I saw you at Punta Arenas airport, I thought Mr. Bertrand had sent you after me."

"So you had Morena fly you to Motunui instead of Easter Island," Joe surmised.

"Yes. I did not want you to intercept me and seize the idol before I could place it back where it belonged. But since you told Iko Hiva you will not take it away again, I decided to tell you the truth."

The Easter Islander took out a handkerchief and dabbed at a cut on the right side of his chin.

"That's a bad cut," Joe observed.

"I got it in a good cause. One of the knife blades protecting the sacred cave nicked me as I reached through the circle to replace the idol on the altar."

He put his handkerchief in his pocket and looked at the Hardys questioningly. "What do you intend to do now?" he asked.

20 *The Final Clue*

Frank and Joe looked at one another. They realized they were thinking the same thing.

"We understand why you gave us such a rough time," Frank spoke up. "We're not about to press charges against you. Or against Morena, either. It was just a foul-up in communications when he conked us at Orongo."

"But you'll have to tell the governor what you told us," Joe pointed out.

"I have no objection to that," Santana stated. "We can go at once."

The three walked over to the governor's residence. Admitted to his office, they found that he already knew from Iko Hiva about the return of the stone idol. Santana then explained that he had put the sculpture back on the altar during the night. He continued with an account of his part in the case. The Hardys added that they were not pressing charges.

"Then that ends it as far as I'm concerned," the governor said. "What are your plans now?"

"I shall stay on Easter Island," Santana replied. "But I hope you will allow Pedro Morena to fly his plane out again. He picked up a charter fare at Punta Arenas. The man wants to go to Santiago."

"Oh, he's the passenger we noticed sitting behind Morena," Frank said. "Why did he come to Easter Island with you if he wanted to go to Santiago?"

Santana shrugged. "He seemed to be afraid of someone. When Pedro told him he had to stop here first, he agreed to come along for the ride just to get out of Punta Arenas. He is an American, by the way."

Suddenly Frank had a hunch. "Julio, what's his name?"

"Sigmund Muller."

Frank and Joe stared at the man. "Muller!" Frank cried out. "He's wanted by the U.S. military for heading a widespread theft ring!"

Now it was Santana's turn to stare. "You mean this man is a criminal?"

"He sure is," Joe declared and quickly told about their mission in the Antarctic.

"Where is Muller now?" the governor demanded after Joe had finished.

"He is waiting for us to pick him up at the Beach Hotel," Santana replied.

"I shall have him arrested at once and brought here," the governor declared.

An hour later, two men with police badges on their shirts brought Sigmund Muller into the governor's office. His eyes bulged when he saw the Hardys and he tried to run, but the two men caught him at the door.

"What a surprise, meeting you here," Joe said. "I thought you were supposed to be in San Diego!"

Muller glared but did not comment.

"I bet you'd feel better if we had fallen into that crevasse on the way to Outpost I," Frank said. "Your pal, Al Ambrose, made another attempt on our lives, but failed. He was arrested and confessed everything!"

"I don't know what you're talking about," Muller said sullenly.

"Your theft ring is exposed and we know you're the leader," Joe told him. "No confession is necessary for your arrest."

Muller shrugged. "You'll have to prove it."

"Don't worry, we will. And I'm sure Admiral Langton will be happy that we found you."

"Governor, is there some way you can hold this man for the U.S. military?" Frank asked. "If you get in touch with Admiral Langton at Byrd Base in Antarctica, he'll arrange for the transfer."

"I certainly can," the governor replied. "We have a jail on the island, even though it is very small."

"Mr. Muller, I'm curious about one thing," Joe said. "Why did you stay in Punta Arenas a whole day, and then take a charter plane to Easter Island?"

Muller realized he was defeated. "I was looking for a friend, who I thought could help me," he replied. "Unfortunately, I didn't find him. When I spotted U.S. military police at the airport, I panicked. I didn't dare book on a commercial airliner, so I found Morena and decided to go with him no matter where he went."

"How'd you ever expect to get back to the United States?" Frank asked.

"I have contacts in Santiago who might have helped."

The governor called Byrd Base and spoke to the admiral, who promised to notify Mr. Hardy that Muller had been found. "I'll submit the necessary extradition papers for Muller and have him picked up," the commander added.

As Muller was led away, the governor turned to the boys. "We would be very happy to entertain you for a while on our island if you'd care to stay," he said.

Frank shook his head. "We still have work to do on the idol case. May I call Mr. Bertrand in Santiago?"

"Of course."

When the young detective spoke to the antique dealer, Bertrand was disturbed to learn that the idol had not been legitimately acquired from Easter Island.

"You'll have to find the Scandinavian collector who sold it to Kim," he told Frank. "I never spoke to the man. I suggest you fly back to New York and talk to my partner."

"If we could figure out who sent Mr. Kimberley that secret message about the sculpture's hiding place, it would help, too," Frank said.

"I questioned my staff, and they deny knowing anything about it," Bertrand said. "If you locate the collector, you might get the answer to this question."

The boys were on the next flight out of Easter Island. They spent the night in Santiago, then continued on to New York.

"I still wonder if Bertrand's on the level," Frank observed.

"So do I," Joe agreed.

"I wonder if he really wants us to find the collector. He seemed uneasy about the whole thing. He might know more than he told us."

"He might be afraid we'll discover that the two of them were in on the theft of the idol," Joe agreed. "The collector stole it, and Bertrand told him to sell it to Kimberley. Later Bertrand stole it from Kimberley. That's one theory anyhow."

"Perhaps he has reason to believe we'll never find the Scandinavian," Frank said. "And he's the only person who can expose the whole thing."

When they arrived at Kennedy Airport, the boys checked into a nearby hotel. The following morning, they phoned Kimberley, who told them to come to his office. They found that he had shaved off his beard.

Frank and Joe recounted the story of the stone idol, ending with the statement that it was permanently back on Easter Island.

"It looks as if the Scandinavian collector who sold you the sculpture is a crook," Frank concluded. "You've got to tell us who he is."

"I tried to find him myself in the meantime," Kimberley said. "Unfortunately, my investigation proves that he does not exist. The man who sold me the idol gave me forged documents and a phony name!"

Agitatedly, Kimberley began to scratch the right side of his chin with his thumb. "I was cheated!" he cried. "Fooled by a thief!"

Suddenly the truth dawned on Frank and Joe at the same time.

"You have a scar in the same place as Julio Santana!" Joe cried out. "He was cut by one of the stone knives in the sacred cave when he put the idol back on the altar. You got cut when you reached in and stole it!"

Kimberley turned ashen white and jumped up from behind his desk. Flinging Joe aside, he tried to push his way past Frank and out the door. But after a short scuffle, the boys subdued him and shoved him back in his chair.

Frank called the police, and soon two officers arrived. They handcuffed the prisoner and informed him of his rights, then Frank gave them the details of their investigation.

When he had finished, he turned to Kimberley.

"You forged the bill of sale for the idol after you returned from Easter Island, and you grew a beard to hide the wound you received from the stone knives!"

"Then you hid the idol in the secret compartment in Bertrand's office before you went to your hotel," Joe took up the story. "The sculpture was not in your handbag when you brought it to your room.

Then you waited to pick up your watch until Bertrand was there so he'd be alone with the bag and could be accused of the theft!"

"Prove it!" Kimberley snarled.

"We will. We know you made up the secret message by cutting words from a newspaper and pasting them on a sheet of South American Antiquities stationery. Then you gave us the note so we'd find the idol and have Bertrand arrested!"

An evil smile curled around Kimberley's lips. "All you have is a harebrained theory. Pure conjecture. I would have no reason to do what you accuse me of."

Suddenly Joe grinned. "But we can prove it. Iko Hiva saw you come up the rope ladder from the sacred cave. He says you were carrying the stone idol, and he'll be glad to identify you in court."

Frank realized his brother was bluffing, and took it one step further. "We also know what your motive was. Mr. Bertrand knows you've been stealing from the company. He'll testify to that. And he can prove it by the records you falsified!"

Kimberley fell right into the trap. His nerve broke and he began to confess.

"I was afraid Bertrand would find out that I faked our financial records," he said, his voice shaking. "So I decided to get rid of him and acquire control of the business."

"That's what you accused *him* of wanting to do," Joe observed.

"I had to ascribe a motive to him," Kimberley muttered, "in order to set him up. When everything was ready, I advertised for a detective because I needed someone who could read the false clues I left in Santiago."

"We followed them at first," Frank admitted. "Then Santana messed everything up for you by snatching the stone idol from us."

"That's when your scheme began to come apart," Joe added. "But it took us a long time to figure out what was going on. The razor did it."

"What razor?" Kimberley grated.

"The one you used to shave your beard."

Kimberley hung his head. "I grew the beard because initially the cut was obvious. But I found it very uncomfortable, so I finally removed it. I didn't think anyone would notice the scar."

"It is so slight that we wouldn't have," Frank admitted, "except you touched it just like Santana touched his fresh cut while we talked to him on Easter Island."

Kimberley shrugged. "Now it'll be easier for Iko Hiva to identify me."

"Actually, it won't," Joe said. "I only made that up in the hope you'd confess."

Kimberley jumped up and let out a string of curses, while the two officers looked admiringly at the boys.

"I also dreamed up the story about Bertrand discovering that you've been stealing from South American Antiquities," Frank added.

Kimberley was so crushed to learn the Hardys had tricked him into a confession that he offered no resistance when the two officers led him away.

The boys looked at each other. Both were relieved that the case was solved, but at the same time they were wondering if they would ever get another assignment that could top the one that took them to such exotic places as Easter Island and Antarctica.

Another mystery, *The Vanishing Thieves*, was to come up soon and would require their best sleuthing skills, even if it did not take them quite as far as the South Pole.

Just then the telephone rang. Frank answered. It was Bertrand from Santiago.

"Where's Kim?" he asked. "How come you're on the line?"

"Mr. Kimberley's at the police station," Frank replied. "He—"

"Good! Make sure he stays there!" Bertrand thundered. "He's been stealing from the firm for a long time. I just found out!"

Frank raised his eyebrows. "You did?"

"That's right. I checked our books. I suspected him ever since you boys told me how he hired you. But I couldn't say so because I had no proof."

"How did you get it?" Frank asked.

"I phoned Kim after you left Easter Island and demanded to know who the Scandinavian collector was. He was so evasive that I decided to go through our financial records with a fine-tooth comb. And there was my proof. He must be arrested at once!"

"Consider it done," Frank replied. "And thanks for the information."

"What information?" Joe asked as Frank hung up.

"Bertrand wants us to know Kimberley's been cheating him for a long time! How about that!"

Don't Miss

THE HARDY BOYS ® MYSTERY STORIES
by Franklin W. Dixon

Night of the Werewolf #59

Mystery of the Samurai Sword #60

The Pentagon Spy #61

The Apeman's Secret #62

The Mummy Case #63

Mystery of Smugglers Cove #64

The Stone Idol #65

The Vanishing Thieves #66

NANCY DREW MYSTERY STORIES ®
by Carolyn Keene

The Triple Hoax #57

The Flying Saucer Mystery #58

The Secret in the Old Lace #59

The Greek Symbol Mystery #60

Plus exciting survival stories in
The Hardy Boys ® Handbook
Seven Stories of Survival
by Franklin W. Dixon with Sheila Link